Also by Jenny Nimmo

Midnight for Charlie Bone
Charlie Bone and the Time Twister
Charlie Bone and the Blue Boa
Charlie Bone and the Castle of Mirrors

The Rinaldi Ring
The Snow Spider Trilogy
Secret Creatures

For younger readers
Matty Mouse
Delilah

Jenny Nimmo

FARM FUN!

THREE BOOKS IN ONE

EGMONT

EGMONT
We bring stories to life

Tatty Apple first published in Great Britain 1984
Beak and Whisker first published in Great Britain 2002
Ill Will, Well Nell first published in Great Britain 2000
Published in one volume as *Farm Fun!* 2007
by Egmont UK Limited
239 Kensington High Street
London W8 6SA

Text copyright © 1984, 2002, 2000 Jenny Nimmo
Tatty Apple illustrations copyright © 2007 Nick Schon
Beak and Whisker illustrations copyright © 2002 Ailie Busby
Ill Will, Well Nell illustrations copyright © 2000
David Wynn Millward

The moral rights of the author and illustrator have been asserted

ISBN 978 1 4052 3305 7

1 3 5 7 9 10 8 6 4 2

www.egmont.co.uk

A CIP catalogue record for this title is available from the British Library

Typeset by Avon DataSet Ltd, Bidford on Avon, Warwickshire
Printed and bound in Great Britain by the CPI Group

Tatty Apple

For Myfanwy, Ianto
and Gwenhwyfar

A Green Rabbit

His first name was Owen and his second name was Owen; everyone in the village called him Owen-Owen, except for his sister, Elin, and she always called him O-O.

Everything in Owen-Owen's land was green; trees, meadows, hedges, the winding river and the mossy stones beside it. Even the slate roofs in his village were green with lichen; everything was green except the Engine, and that was as red as a poppy. So,

1

living, as he did, in this green land, Owen should not have been surprised when he saw a green rabbit, but then he would never have seen the rabbit if it had not been for the Engine.

Owen lived with his mother, his sister and his brothers, in a high little house in the village of Llanibont. His father had died a year before. Mr Owen had worked on an oil rig. One day, just before he was due to come home, he fell into the sea. No one ever found him. Although he seldom saw him Owen had thought his father very wonderful and brave. He missed his dad's summer visits when they would fish side by side in the green river; he missed him at chestnut time, and at Christmas, when there would be an electric train or a box of soldiers, rattling in one of dad's big pockets. But in spring, Owen missed his father most of all.

It was in spring, only a year ago, that Owen and his father had walked down to the station together to admire the Engine. They had not been for a ride then, there had been so many treats to cram into so short a time. But Mr Owen had made a promise. 'Next time we'll go on the train, Owen-Owen, just you and me, all the way to Llyndu and back.' A promise that could not be kept.

Now spring had come again and when Owen looked out of his bedroom window, he never noticed the tractors bumbling down the twisty lanes, the milk cart meeting the bread van on the hill. The Engine had come out of its winter shed and sat in the little station waiting for passengers, and the Engine was the only thing that Owen saw or thought about.

But Mrs Owen would not let her eldest son ride on the train by himself, and that is why he was lying on his bed, one Saturday May morning, feeling angry and sad.

'I must go on the train, I must! I must go on the train, I must, I must, I must!' said Owen to the wallpaper dragons climbing round his bedroom.

He jumped off his bed and ran downstairs. Mam and Elin were in the kitchen, arguing about chickens again. Tom and Huwie were fighting in the sitting-room. There was so much noise.

Owen burst into the kitchen. 'Mam, can I go on the train today?'

Mrs Owen sighed. 'Not by yourself,

Owen-Owen, not until you're older. If Elin will go with you . . .'

'No thanks!' said Elin. 'The seats are hard. It gives you ever such a shaking, my bottom was blue last time.'

'I'll get you anything you want, if you come,' said Owen. 'Well, almost anything.'

'A red hen?' asked Elin.

'Yes, yes, a red hen, if I can find one.'

'No,' said Mam. 'The garden will be ruined, all that scratching and pecking.'

'Oh, Mam, come on,' cried Elin. 'Just think, a big brown egg for breakfast, every day.'

'I'll find one, Elin,' said Owen. 'If you'll come on the train with me?'

'Mr Evans, up at Ty Uchaf, has one. I know, because Ceris Jones was there with her mam for some jumble, and she peeped in the yard. There were six lovely red hens and some chicks too and . . .'

'I can't go in there!' said Owen, aghast.

'Scared?'

'No.'

'You're frightened,' said Elin. 'Well, I won't come on the train with you.'

'I'll go to Mr Evans,' said Owen. 'I'm not scared.'

But he was. Mr Evans lived by himself in a tumble-down building in the hills. He rarely came to the village, and if he did, he spoke not a word except to ask for groceries. He reared his lambs, sheared his sheep, harvested and ploughed his windy hillside alone, and no one knew how he went on, season after season.

Ty Uchaf was the last place in the world that Owen would have chosen to visit, but he longed to go on the train.

'I haven't agreed about the hen yet,' said Mrs Owen.

'But, Mam, the lovely eggs!' cried Elin.

'And the train,' added her brother.

Mrs Owen put down her darning and folded her arms. 'Go on then, Owen-Owen,' she said softly, 'get a paper carrier from the cupboard, a strong one mind, you don't want Elin's red hen flying off, and be back by tea-time.'

Owen ran to the hall cupboard, pulled out the biggest bag he could find, and dashed through the front door.

'Good luck!' called Elin.

The last thing he heard was his mother laughing and it made him feel good. He knew that he would be successful.

When he reached the path up to Ty

Uchaf, however, it was a different matter. In Llanibont it had been too warm to put on a jersey, but here there was the beginning of a cold wind, and tiny drops of rain flew in his face. He could see Ty Uchaf above him; soon, when he began to climb the steepest part of the hill, if would disappear, until he was almost beside the gate. He walked through a ring of oak trees, trying not to crush the bluebells that clustered at his feet,

and he thought that he must remember to pick some for Mam, on his return.

As Owen climbed upwards the wind became stronger and by the time he had reached the grey wall round Ty Uchaf, his ears and nose were stinging with the cold. He walked up to the front door but found there was no handle, nor a bell of any sort. He began to creep, rather reluctantly, round the side of the building. It was a strange, forbidding place, so lonely and so old. The wind moaned against the dark walls like the voices of ancient men, gone a thousand years ago. Suddenly, he came to the end of the house and found himself looking up into a pair of fierce black eyes.

'Who are you?' growled Mr Evans, and he banged the ground with a stout black stick.

Owen took a step backwards. 'I'm Owen-Owen,' he said, 'from Llanibont, and I've come for a red hen. My sister, Elin, wants one, and if I don't get it I can't go on the train.'

Mr Evans glared at Owen. His thin lips twisted, but not in a smile. The boy felt cold; he wrapped his arms, comfortingly, around himself and asked timidly, 'Do you know the red Engine, Mr Evans, down in Llanibont, or . . . or don't you hear it, all the way up here?'

'Of course I know the Engine,' Mr Evans said gruffly. He rubbed the side of his long nose with his forefinger and muttered, 'Better come with me.' He walked away from the boy into the farmyard where six red hens pecked at tiny specks of hayseed blowing round their feet.

Mr Evans leant on his stick and smiled at his hens. 'She's got good sense, your sister,' he said. 'Hens are good to have about, very good. Which one do you want?'

'I don't know,' said Owen. 'Which is the best?'

'I'll not give you my best hen,' shouted Mr Evans, beating his stick upon the ground again. The hens, startled, began to scatter but the old man grabbed the slowest and thrust it at Owen.

'Oh, thank you! Thank you!' murmured Owen, clutching the terrified hen to his chest. 'How much is it, then?'

'Nothing!' grunted Mr Evans. 'Go away! Go!'

At that moment a gust of wind blew
through the farmyard. Slates clattered off
the barn roof; straw and dust flew into the
air and an empty bucket bounced over the
farmyard cobbles with a deafening clatter.
During this commotion the tall, grey
presence of Mr Evans vanished, whether
into the barn, the house or thin air, Owen
never knew.

When the wind had blown itself out of
the farmyard, Owen tucked his red hen into
the carrier-bag but, turning to run away, a
small sound on the ground made him
step back, carefully. There, at
his feet, sat a rabbit, a small
green-eyed rabbit with
shiny green fur. Not brown,
black or even grey, but
definitely green.

Without knowing why, or how, he did it, Owen picked up the rabbit and thrust it into his bag, on top of the red hen. Then he ran, ran, ran, faster than the wind, down the slipping, sliding, stony path and away from Ty Uchaf. He did not forget to gather an armful of bluebells when he passed through the oak grove, and he piled the flowers in the bag that was now bursting with movement.

Owen slowed his pace when he reached the village. He did not want to arouse suspicion. For reasons that he could not explain, he did not want anyone to know what he had in his brown carrier-bag.

On the bridge he met Mostyn Mathias. No one in Llanibont liked Mostyn. His father ran the Blue Boar pub; he was a widower, but a merry man and he could never understand why Mostyn was mean and miserable, and liked to bully children smaller than himself.

'Where have you been, Owen-Owen?' Mostyn asked. He despised Owen for looking so happy.

'Shopping!' muttered Owen.

Mostyn was fourteen, taller and stronger than Owen. The older boy came very close and, for a moment, it seemed as though he would snatch the precious bag away, but Owen jumped nimbly to one side and ran over the bridge before Mostyn could touch him.

He could feel Mostyn's eyes on his back as he ran up the hill to his house. When he burst into the kitchen he was quite breathless. Mam and Elin were there, and Tom and Huwie were sitting at the table with boiled eggs and bread and butter before them. Owen strode into the middle of the kitchen and gently turned the paper bag upside down. The red hen flapped her way up to the windowsill, clucking loudly; bluebells tumbled at Mrs Owen's feet, and then out leapt the green rabbit.

Tom and Huwie were speechless for once, but Elin cried, 'Thank you, O-O! Thank you, thank you! What a beautiful red hen,' and she ran and took the grumbling bird in her arms.

'Thank you for the flowers, Owen-Owen,' Mrs Owen said, but she was looking at the green rabbit.

'Funny rabbit,' cried Huwie, banging his spoon on the table.'

'It's green,' shouted Tom excitedly.

'Not really green,' said Elin, rather scornful. 'He's green and brown, like an apple that's waited too long, a tatty old apple.' She hugged her hen tighter and began to dance round the table. 'Oh, she's lovely, lovely, my hen,' she cried. 'I shall call her Poppy, because she's red, red, red as a poppy.'

'What'll you call your rabbit, Owen-Owen?' asked Tom.

Owen hesitated. 'Tatty Apple, I suppose,' he murmured, 'because he's like an apple that's waited too long.'

'He's certainly a very unusual rabbit,' said Mrs Owen.

But none of them realised just how unusual Tatty Apple really was.

Moving Objects

It was decided that the Great Train Ride would take place the following Saturday. If it had not been for Tatty Apple Owen would have spent the week in an agony of suspense; as it was he had far too much on his mind. He had to find wood, wire, bolts and nails with which to make Tatty Apple a secure hutch and run. He was also expected to make Elin a hen-coop for Poppy. Owen spent half an hour secretly consulting a paperback on chickens, on one of Mrs

Price-the-Papers' back shelves, and then went home to construct a rather rickety little hut beneath the apple tree.

For a few days life was perfect. Elin cooed happily to her Poppy, from the moment she arrived back from school until she went to bed. No brown eggs appeared though. Tom and Huwie were almost quiet, watching the antics of the green rabbit in its run, and Owen banged away with his tool-set in every spare minute, until he put in the final nail, only a night before the great day.

Elin was reluctant to leave Poppy on the first whole day they would have spent together, but tore herself away to put on her new Saturday dress.

On Saturday afternoon, all his tasks accomplished, Owen checked his pocket money, spat on his shoes to wipe the dust away – the Engine-driver might see them – and called his sister.

They were about to open the front door when there was a shriek from Mam. 'Rabbit's out! Owen-Owen, catch that rabbit!'

Owen held his breath and gazed helplessly at Elin.

'Better go,' said Elin. 'We've plenty of time.'

They ran back through the house to the back garden. The rabbit-hutch door was open. Owen clutched his hair in despair. It would take ten minutes, at least, to discover how Tatty Apple had opened it. However, he had an idea. Scooping up the green rabbit, he ran to the tool-shed, pulled the old guinea-pig cage from a shelf and stuffed

Tatty Apple inside.

'It's all right, Mam, I've fixed it,' he shouted.

'You can't put him in that, it's too small,' said Elin.

'I'll have to,' Owen replied. 'Come on!'

They raced past Mam, standing suspicious by the kitchen sink, and were about to run out of the front door when Owen realised he was still carrying the guinea-pig cage. He ran back to the sitting-room and dumped the cage in a corner by the sofa.

Sometimes Elin liked to hold Owen's hand, and today was one of those times. Speeding down the hill they laughed until they thought they would burst. Owen laughed because he was so happy and Elin laughed because everyone they passed giggled at Owen, everyone except Mrs Price-the-Papers, who never laughed at anyone, she was always so busy reading the sad, bad news of the day.

They reached the station with five minutes to spare, for buying tickets, crisps, a pencil for Mam and two postcards of the Engine, one for Tom and one for Huwie. Then they boarded the first carriage.

It was an old train but the big windowpanes sparkled and the wooden seats shone like new. At either end of the carriages there were small open balconies with a half-door that opened on to the boarding steps. The children decided to stay on the balcony.

The best thing about the journey was not the hissing of the steam, the rattling and the shaking, but the things that they could see. On one side there was a bald hill and a derelict farm, on the other a deep, green, secret river that they never saw from the village or the road. A family of ducks clattered out of the reeds, a motionless heron watched and listened from his stony pool. A decaying boat bobbed against the rocks.

The train slowed down for they were ascending the hill to Castell Coch, the red castle; a mound of ancient stones and soft grass, a thousand years old, or more. Many a bloody battle had been fought over those stones, but today Castell Coch was a peaceful place of bright flowers and grazing sheep.

The red castle swept away and they were going down, fast, fast to the valley of the deserted watermill. The sun never shone here. The mill was old and cold, the base of its thick, grey walls, green from the river in flood. Owen remembered the sad stories that the villagers told about the mill in flood, and suddenly he found that they were in the darkness of the sooty tunnel that took them out of the valley. They emerged into a field of golden buttercups.

Owen watched the fireman shovelling coal into the furnace. He gazed at Jo, the driver; his face red from the glowing coals, his forearms thick as oak branches. How good it must be to drive a steam engine!

They were back in Llanibont long before Owen was ready to leave the train. He wished his father had been with him, but Elin was not such a bad companion.

'It was all right, wasn't it?' he asked his sister, as they left the station.

'It was pretty good,' Elin admitted. 'Could be I was too young to appreciate it before.'

'Could be,' Owen agreed.

He knew something had happened at home before they reached the gate. They could hear Tom sobbing, but it was not just that, it was an eerie feeling that something very unusual had occurred.

Elin opened the front door and they beheld Tom spread-eagled on the hall floor, his face buried in the rug.

'Why are you crying, Tom?' Owen knelt beside his brother.

Tom wiped his nose. 'Mam says I moved her things and I didn't,' he sobbed.

'What things?' Elin asked.

'In the sitting-room. The mirror, and her little jug, and – and all the other things.'

Elin looked into the sitting-room. The big mirror above the fireplace was crooked and balanced, precariously, upon the top of its thick wooden frame were a small china jug, a glass cat and a photograph of their grandmother, Nain, in a silver frame.

'What a very peculiar thing to do,' Elin

murmured.

Tom got up and joined them in the doorway. 'I didn't do it,' he repeated.

Owen regarded the tiny objects on the mirror, sparkling in a rosy light from the evening sun. Tom did not always tell the truth, but this time Owen believed him.

'Let's go and see Mam,' said Elin.

Mrs Owen was sitting in the kitchen with Huwie on her lap. Huwie was sipping a cup of milk. 'Owen-Owen,' he cried delightedly. 'Elin-Elin!'

'Hullo, Huwie, here's a picture for you,' said Owen, remembering his presents from the station, 'and one for Tom.'

'Tom has been a naughty boy,' said Mam.

'We saw,' said Elin.

'Tom says he didn't do it,' Owen felt he

had to stand up for his brother. 'Here's a pencil for you, Mam, with a train on it, see. Thanks for letting us go. It was just great.'

'Good,' Mrs Owen smiled. 'Now perhaps you'll help me put things right.' She lifted Huwie down and they all went into the sitting-room.

'It's such a very silly thing to do,' said Mam, pushing an armchair beneath the mirror. She stood on the chair and lifted her arms, but she had to stand on tiptoe to reach the jug, the cat and the photograph of Nain. She handed them down, one by one, to Elin who replaced them on the mantelpiece.

'Tom couldn't have done it, Mam,' Owen muttered. 'He couldn't reach that high; he's much too small.'

'SOMEONE moved my things,' cried

Mam. 'It was a very silly, naughty thing to do.'

No one said much during tea. Owen told Tom and Huwie about the train, and Huwie got very excited, but then everyone else went back to thinking about the strange happening in the sitting-room.

Tom and Huwie went to bed after tea. Elin and Owen watched television for a while, and then Elin said she would go and say 'good-night' to Poppy.

Owen was suddenly reminded of his rabbit. 'Tatty Apple!' he exclaimed. 'Poor rabbit, shut up in that cage, and we never even noticed him.'

He ran to the sitting-room and flung open the door. The first thing he saw was the grandfather clock. He saw it first because sitting right on top of it were the china jug, the glass cat and the photograph of Nain. They had been moved again.

'Oh no!' gasped Owen. He picked up the rabbit in its cage and went into the kitchen. Mam was hanging mugs on the dresser.

'Mam,' said Owen quietly. 'It's happened again. The jug, the cat and the photograph. They're on top of the grandfather clock this time.'

His mother frowned. 'All right, Owen-Owen,' she said. 'I'll see to it later.'

'You don't really think it's one of us doing it, do you?' asked Owen.

'No,' replied Mrs Owen. 'No, I don't

think it is.' And then she added, 'I wish your dad was here.'

'So do I, Mam,' said Owen. He ran into the garden, fetched his tool-kit from the shed and secured the rabbit-hutch door again.

'Good-night, Tatty Apple,' said Owen, placing the green rabbit into its hutch. 'See you tomorrow!'

Elin had already kissed her red hen and put her to bed. Owen followed his sister into the house and up the stairs.

'Elin,' whispered Owen, as he reached his bedroom door. 'It happened again. The jug, the cat and the photograph of Nain. They're on top of the clock this time. Who d'you think did it?'

'I don't know,' Elin replied. 'I don't believe in ghosts, it's very peculiar though.

It could have been Tom, he's clever.'

Owen went into the bedroom and shut the door. Tom had not moved Mam's things, of that he was certain. But who had?

Owen climbed into bed, thought about the green rabbit, the grandfather clock and the crooked mirror, and fell asleep.

Magic at Night

As soon as he awoke, the following morning, Owen climbed on to Tom's bed and looked out of the window. He saw Poppy strutting about her run; he saw Bobby, Mrs Price's black cat, watching Poppy from the garden wall, but he could not see Tatty Apple. The rabbit hutch was empty.

Owen bounced off Tom's bed, and without bothering to put on his slippers, ran down into the garden. The wire on Tatty

Apple's hutch was still secure, but the door was open and the bolt drawn back; someone or something had opened the rabbit hutch from outside.

'No! No! No!' Owen yelled at the top of his voice. 'No! No! No! Tatty Apple's gone!'

In a few seconds he was joined by Tom and Elin, both in their pyjamas. They searched the garden, turning over every empty flower-pot, every bucket, box and board. They even looked in the water-butt, but the green rabbit was nowhere to be found.

At length they trailed in for breakfast and broke the news to Mrs Owen. She did not seem too upset by the rabbit's disappearance, but, seeing the look in Owen's eyes, she pulled her eldest son towards her. 'You can always get another rabbit, Owen-Owen,' she said gently. 'I've seen really beautiful rabbits in the pet shop in Llyndu, big white ones with black ears, and black ones, and . . .'

'Never, never a green one, I bet,' said Owen.

'No, never,' Mrs Owen admitted.

'How could he just vanish, Mam?' cried Owen. 'There's a wall all round the garden, and who would open the hutch and take him, no one knew he was there?'

His mother hesitated, then she said, 'Perhaps it has something to do with all those strange happenings last night, the jug, the cat and the photo of Nain.'

'It wasn't me!' cried Tom.

'No, I don't believe it was you, Tom,' said Mrs Owen. 'And if anything strange happens again I shall tell Davy Wynn.'

Davy Wynn was the village policeman;
he was more than that, he kept things
straight in Llanibont. Davy Wynn was kind
and he was a good friend when you needed
one, but he was six feet four without his
boots on, and he had a voice like the echo
in a mountain cave. And when he was
angry you would do anything to make him
happy again.

They ate their cornflakes in silence,
each one secretly imagining the punishment
that might await the 'person' who had been
interfering with Mam's things.

After breakfast Mrs Owen dressed Tom
and Huwie and took them for a walk. Elin
went into the garden to look for a brown
egg, but Owen did not leave the kitchen.
He sat and gazed at a blue bowl of oranges
on the table, pretending he could see a

rabbit hiding behind every fruit. He shut
his eyes and rested his head on the table so
that he should see the rabbits more clearly.

Something made him lift his head. The
bowl of oranges was moving. It drifted
gracefully to the end of the table and
slowly, very slowly, rose into the air, hovered
a little and continued its ascent towards the
ceiling; here the blue bowl circled the light
a few times, then floated to the highest shelf
on the kitchen dresser, where it came to
rest. Not one orange had moved a
millimetre.

Owen swung round, expecting to see
Elin holding a piece of cotton or wire. But
there was no one else in the kitchen. He
scanned the room and saw the kitchen
cupboard, the sink, Nain's old oak chair, the
blue pedal-bin, and beside the pedal-bin – a

green rabbit!

'Tatty Apple,' cried Owen. He ran to
the little rabbit and picked him up. 'Oh,
Tatty! Tatty!' he said, stroking the silky
green fur. 'Where have you been? Did you
see the magic?'

Forgetting Mam and hygiene, Owen put
the green rabbit on the table in the midst of
the clean plates and shining cutlery. Tatty
Apple did a very strange thing then. He
drew himself into a tight little ball and
closed his eyes.

A knife flew across the buttercup cloth
and clattered to the floor. A fork hovered in
mid-air and dropped back to the table. The
cereal bowls circled the table colliding into
mugs and plates.

Owen jumped up, his chair crashed
over on to the stone floor. 'What's

happening?' he shouted, and then, quietly, 'Tatty Apple, did you do that?'

The little green rabbit opened one eye.

'If . . . if you did, can you bring the oranges back, please?'

Tatty Apple looked at Owen. He drew in his paws and hunched himself into a ball, tighter and tighter. He stared at Owen out of one eye until Owen felt he would drown in the dark greenness of it; and then, slowly, very slowly, the blue bowl floated off the top shelf of the dresser and descended slowly, very slowly, until it rested in the middle of the table beside the rabbit.

'Tatty Apple, you are a very marvellous animal,' Owen murmured. 'But how am I . . . what am I going to tell them? Perhaps

I shan't tell anyone, except Elin.'

The little rabbit hopped towards Owen and nibbled his finger. Owen stroked the rabbit's soft nose and Tatty Apple closed his eyes and crept into the boy's arms.

When Elin came in from the garden half an hour later, she found her brother still sitting at the kitchen table in his pyjamas, whispering to himself.

'You'd better get dressed, O-O,' Elin said. 'Mam will be back soon.' Then she saw the rabbit. 'You found him, O-O!' she cried. 'Where was he?'

'He just came back,' said Owen.

'I'll put him in the hutch,' said Elin. 'You get dressed quickly now, or Mam will be cross.'

Owen handed his rabbit to Elin. He wanted to tell his sister about the bowl of oranges, but he felt that the time was not right.

'You probably didn't bolt the door properly,' said Elin as she disappeared into the garden.

'I did,' muttered Owen. He heard his brothers shouting as they came up the hill and he ran upstairs just before Mrs Owen opened the front door and the two little boys tumbled into the hall.

Tom and Huwie were delighted to find that the green rabbit had returned. Tom wanted to make it an excuse for a party but Mam insisted that the freshly baked cake should remain whole until tea time.

To Owen's surprise, Tatty Apple stayed within his hutch, contentedly munching the weeds and vegetables that were almost continuously thrust into him. Knowing that the rabbit could move the bolt on his door without any difficulty, Owen sat in the garden all day, watching him. He came in for his sausage and chips, but ran out again before his usual second helping, even refusing the ice-cream treat to follow.

Mrs Owen was surprised. Elin was suspicious.

After tea, when Tom and Huwie were bathed and tucked up in bed, Owen declined a game of cards with Elin, kissed his mother 'good-night' and crept out into the garden.

Tatty Apple had gone. Owen closed the hutch door and went back into the kitchen. This time he did not mention the rabbit's disappearance. 'Night, Mam,' he said. 'Just been to see the rabbit.'

Owen climbed the stairs and went into his room. He did not undress. He sat on his bed for a long time, listening to his brothers' soft breathing. He wondered if he had seen Tatty Apple for the last time. He did not think so.

When it was nearly dark, he got up, opened the door as quietly as he could and tiptoed over the passage to Elin's bedroom. It was a tiny room, a cupboard really, so she always left her door open. Owen peeped in. 'Elin, are you asleep?' he whispered.

Elin groaned. 'Yes, I was, almost,' she grumbled. 'What is it?'

Owen stepped into the room and sat on Elin's bed. 'Tatty Apple's gone again,' he said.

'Oh, I'm sorry,' Elin yawned.

'But it's not just that. He opened the hutch door all by himself.'

'Don't be silly,' said Elin. She slid down under the blankets and turned away from Owen.

'It's true! It's true!' Owen jumped up and grasped his sister's shoulder. 'He can do more than that. He can move things just by . . . thinking.'

Elin began to shriek with laughter and then, suddenly, she stopped. A small shape with long ears had appeared in the doorway.

'Tatty Apple,' breathed Owen.

Elin put on her bedside light. The little rabbit's eyes glittered. He hopped into the

room and raised his head, his nose twitching.

'Oh, it's all nonsense,' said Elin. 'He can't move things at all, he's just a silly old rabbit.'

The bedside table fell over, and the light went out. Something, a book, hit Owen's head, then flew into Elin's face. She screamed. Her pillow rose into the air and thumped back on to the bed. A pair of shoes clattered across the floor. Elin's bed reared up on two legs and crashed back on

to the floorboards. Then there was silence.

'Will you . . . t . . . take Tatty Apple away now, O-O?' Elin whispered. 'I believe you. He's a magical rabbit, but I don't want him in my room if . . . if he's going to do things like that.' She drew the blankets up tight to her neck.

Owen picked up the table and the lamp, then he pushed Elin's pillow behind her head. 'Good-night, Elin,' he said kindly, and, tucking the green rabbit under one arm, he crept on to the landing.

The kitchen door was ajar and a soft light illuminated the staircase. Someone was singing on the radio and his mother joined in, now and again, as she made biscuits. The smell was delicious.

Owen looked into one of the rabbit's deep green eyes. 'Better sleep with me tonight, Tatty Apple,' he said.

He put the rabbit under his bed, undressed and jumped in. A few moments later Mrs Owen came upstairs and peeped into the room. 'Are you awake, Owen-Owen?' she asked. 'There was a terrible noise up here just now.'

'I dropped a book, Mam,' replied Owen.

'Only a book? Good-night, my love. Go to sleep now!' she closed the door.

Owen listened to his mother's footsteps receding down the passage. He heard her door close. An owl hooted outside the window.

He put his hand down and gently stroked the rabbit's nose.

Tatty Apple did not move. He seemed to be fast asleep.

Trouble

It was good to have Elin share the secret.
On warm evenings Owen would put
Tatty Apple in his brown bag and brother
and sister would carry it down to the woods
beside the river. When they were sure no
one was near, they would set the bag down
and release the green rabbit.

At first Tatty Apple did nothing but
scurry hither and thither, chewing a piece
of grass, a twig; scratching the dry earth
and dancing in the air, but after a few visits

to the river bank the rabbit seemed to understand that Elin and Owen expected something of him. They were sitting on the bank one evening, throwing tiny stones into the water when, suddenly one of Owen's pebbles sprang back out of the water and fell, with a thud, beside him. Elin laughed delightedly and Owen knew that the magic had begun again.

Elin picked a bunch of primroses and placed them between the rabbit's ears. They floated into the air above her, and then dropped into her dark hair.

'You're all stars, Elin,' cried Owen, as she fell back, giggling into the grass.

That afternoon the green rabbit played gentle, funny tricks. Owen's shoes flew into a tree; Elin's white socks drifted over the river, like a dove, and the carrier-bag filled

itself with twigs, becoming a giant
hedgehog rolling through the trees.

'He's so wonderful, O-O!' breathed
Elin. 'Shouldn't we share his magic with
someone else?'

'No!' said Owen fiercely.

'Not even Mam?'

'No! Not yet, anyway!'

Elin said nothing. She gathered a
handful of tiny blue speedwell and
scattered them at the edge of the water.
Tatty Apple was lying on his side, dozing,
so they thought, but suddenly the blue
flowers began to move; one after the other
they lifted themselves from the dry grass
and, hesitantly, joined together in a tiny
ring that whirled out into the last ray of sun
above the water.

They walked home in silence, each one

wondering about the dancing flowers, the colours and the patterns that Tatty Apple had made.

On Saturday mornings the two eldest Owens often did the shopping for their mother. There was a lot to collect for the family of five, and to make things easier, they each had a list and a shopping bag, though Elin always carried the money, in a large leather purse tied to her belt.

One Saturday, on impulse, Owen popped Tatty Apple into his shopping bag before running to catch up with his sister, who had already left the house.

Their first visit was to the grocer's where Mrs Owen's

regular order was ready for the children to collect. Mr Watkins, the grocer, gave them an apple each and, after exchanging news of Huwie's latest escapade with that of Mr Watkins' youngest grandson, the children moved on to the paper shop.

Elin gave Owen three silver coins and he laid them on Mrs Price's counter.

'Well, what's that for, Owen-Owen?' asked Mrs Price.

'You know. Mam's papers,' said Owen.

'And what papers are those?' Mrs Price looked especially pink and her hair was particularly fuzzy.

Owen sighed and consulted his list.

'Woman's Day and the one for the telly,' said Elin.

'It's about time your brother knew what he came for,' said Mrs Price.

'Have you had a hair-do, Mrs Price?' Owen enquired.

'None of your business,' snapped Mrs Price and pushed the magazines into Owen's shopping bag. She didn't notice the dark green eye that stared out at her through a hole in the bag, nor did she see a large box of chocolates slide gracefully off a shelf and drop into that same bag, as Owen left the shop.

The next visit was easy. Mr Humphreys, the butcher, was friendly. He always knew what the Owens wanted, and he was so busy chatting about the weather, his children and his cat, that he never saw the four fresh chickens, in the window, jump on to a dish of mince. Mrs James, who came in later, noticed the muddle though, and asked who had been in before her.

Meanwhile Elin and Owen had reached
Bowen's Bakery. Elin read out her list while
Owen sniffed around happily. The smell of
fresh bread always made him feel hungry.
He eyed the iced buns in the window. Elin
handed him two loaves of bread. Owen
hesitated before putting them into his bag,
he could see Tatty Apple's nose twitching
between a packet of tea and a tin of baked
beans. Owen put the bread into Elin's bag.

'What did you do that for?' asked Elin.

'My bag's full,' Owen replied.

'No it isn't!'

When Mrs Bowen leant over the
counter to referee, a large cake decorated
with pink roses, took a leap from a stand
beside the door and landed in the passage
at the back of the shop. No one saw it. The
pink cake took another leap and dropped

into the muddy back yard. It was Polly Pugh's thirteenth-birthday cake.

Mrs Bowen sorted out the bread problem. 'One loaf into Elin's bag and one into Owen-Owen's,' she said.

Owen tucked his loaf behind the orange juice, where the green rabbit would not immediately sniff it out. 'Let's go down to the river before we go back,' he suggested.

Elin was tempted. 'Mam might worry if we're late with the meat,' she said.

'Come on, just for a few minutes,' begged Owen. He took his sister's hand and began to pull her down the street towards the bridge.

'O-O, you haven't got your rabbit in there, have you?' Elin eyed Owen's shopping bag suspiciously.

But before Owen had time to reply
there came a shriek from the top of the hill.
Mrs Price had emerged from her shop and
was galloping towards them.

'Thief! Thief!' she cried. 'I'll have you,
Owen-Owen. Stealing my best box of
chocolates, is it?'

'I never,' cried Owen.

'You villain!' Mrs Price shook her fist.

The sight of Mrs Price with her hair all

a-fuzz and her fist shaking sent Owen
fleeing away down the street.

'I'm sure you're mistaken, Mrs Price,'
Elin shouted over her shoulder, and she too
began to run.

There came another shout, high-
pitched and awful. Elin and Owen stopped
and turned. Mrs Price had stumbled over
Mr Humphreys' mad, bad little terrier,
Fred, and now she came rolling down the

middle of the steep road towards them. It was a terrifying thing to see; Mrs Price's pink petticoat all muddied, big pink legs kicking, and the words she was screaming, too dreadful for tender ears.

The children ran, half-weeping, half-choking with silent laughter. They ran until the pain in Owen's side forced him to drop to the ground. The carrier-bag burst open and out tumbled the green rabbit and a large box of chocolates.

'Oh no!' gasped Owen. He hastily gathered the rest of his shopping together and bundled it into the bag, but he left the shiny box of chocolates in the middle of the road. Tatty Apple had vanished.

Owen glanced back up the road. Mrs Price had managed to pull herself up on Dai Jones's tractor, which was rumbling up the hill rather slowly, and now she resumed her pursuit, faster and fiercer than ever.

Owen tucked the broken bag under his arm and followed Elin over the bridge. He heard Mrs Price pounce on the chocolates with the triumphant cry of a warrior chieftain. At last, the dreadful clatter of her spiky shoes ceased, and the screams of vengeance died to a mad muttering.

He found Elin crouching in a clump of elderflower bushes beneath the bridge.

'I suppose it was Tatty Apple?' Elin glared at her brother.

'Must have been,' admitted Owen. 'I found the chocolates in my shopping bag.'

'Why ever did you bring him shopping?'

'I thought he'd like it, just for a change,' mumbled Owen.

'Thought he'd like it?' Elin got to her

feet and shook out her skirt. 'Come on, O-O. I just hope Mrs Price isn't going to make trouble.'

'Let's go home the back way,' said Owen. 'I don't want to go through the village again.'

'It'll take ages and Mam will worry,' Elin replied. 'But I know what you mean. Come on, we'd better get going, fast.'

The back way meant running along the bank until they reached the bridge where the little train crossed the river, then climbing up through Dai Jones's fields and into the woods that covered the hills above Llanibont. It took them three miles out of their way and, even though they ran when they could, and climbed faster than they could remember having climbed, they were an hour late for lunch.

Mrs Owen was sitting at the big table when the children burst into the kitchen. Her eyes were very bright and her face flushed. 'Mr Wynn wants to see you, Owen-Owen,' she said quietly. 'He's in the sitting-room.'

Owen looked at Elin, then he walked slowly out of the kitchen and down the hall. He turned the handle of the sitting-room door and peeped inside. Davy Wynn was sitting in an armchair facing him.

'Come in, Owen-Owen,' said Davy Wynn, 'and close the door behind you.'

Owen slammed the door, walked over to the fireplace and began to chew his thumb.

'Now then, are you going to tell me about the chocolates and the chickens and Polly Pugh's birthday cake?' asked the policeman gruffly.

'Chickens?' enquired Owen.

'And cake!'

'And cake?' Owen repeated.

'Don't act silly, Owen-Owen. They found Polly's birthday cake in the back yard, covered in mud, just after you had left the bakery. Mr Humphreys' fresh chickens all over the mince, and you the last one to leave his shop. As for the chocolates, well, Mrs Price saw you, didn't she?' Davy Wynn's glance was severe but there was no anger in his voice.

'The chocolates, yes. But I don't know anything about the chickens and the birthday cake,' said Owen defiantly. 'I just found the chocolates in my bag, they must have fallen in, or something.'

'Your mam says some strange things have been happening in this house. Have you been playing tricks on your mam, Owen-Owen?' Davy Wynn sounded almost kind now.

'No, I never!' Owen shouted. 'Mam knows I haven't, she . . .' he faltered, for while he had been speaking, Davy Wynn's hat, which had been lying on a stool beside him, had taken off and was now flying through the air towards a bookcase behind him.

It was evident that Tatty Apple had reached the house before them and had lodged himself in a cosy nook somewhere in the sitting-room. Owen was suddenly overcome with a great desire to rid himself of his secret, to reveal the real culprit. It would have been so easy: the hat was still in mid-air, he could have said, 'Look, Mr Wynn! Look at your hat! See, it is the green rabbit who is doing these things, not I!' But he could not betray his friend. Instead he clasped his hands and silently begged Tatty Apple to send the hat back.

The hat came to rest on the top shelf of the bookcase.

Owen closed his eyes. There was a long silence and then he suddenly felt a heavy hand on his shoulder. He looked up and found the policeman staring down at him.

'You miss your dad, boy, don't you? He was a fine man, your dad; he was special wasn't he?' Davy Wynn's voice was gentler than Owen had ever heard it. 'Look here,

Owen-Owen, you've been a bad lad, but you won't be foolish again, will you?' Davy Wynn patted the boy's shoulder. 'I'll be going now but if you feel a bit down, come and have a chat. I'm a friend, Owen-Owen, will you remember that?'

'I'll remember,' said Owen. He wished Davy Wynn would stay longer now. There were so many things that he wanted to talk about.

'Tell your mam everything's all right. She's a fine woman, and I don't like to see her worried.' Davy Wynn looked down for his hat.

'It's over there, Mr Wynn!' Owen pointed a rather shaky finger at the bookcase.

The policeman looked puzzled. 'Could have sworn I left it on the stool,' he

muttered. Then, retrieving his hat, he turned to Owen, winked and was gone.

The door had hardly closed when Owen became aware of a loud scuffling from under the chenille tablecloth. He rushed over to the table, flung up the cloth and found Tatty Apple chewing steadily through the velvet fronds that hung down over the other side of the table.

Owen grabbed the little rabbit and pulled him out. He wanted to hit Tatty Apple, to hurt him, punish him for the trouble he had caused, and then he remembered the dancing flowers, the socks that flew like a dove, and his eyes filled with tears.

Lifting Tatty Apple up to his face he pressed his cheek against the soft fur. 'You did it, you clever rabbit,' Owen sobbed. 'You're cleverer than anyone, aren't you?'

He had not cried since his father was drowned, Elin had shed enough tears for all of them. But now he had allowed his tears to fall, he could not stop them.

'What's the matter, O-O?' Elin had come quietly into the room and stood staring at her brother in concern. 'What did Davy Wynn say?'

'Nothing,' Owen sobbed angrily, 'and he doesn't know anything.' Then, shoving Elin back against the door, he rushed upstairs and flung himself on the bed.

He remained in his room all afternoon, angry with Mrs Price, angry with himself, and, most of all, angry with Tatty Apple. Tatty Apple to whom he clung so desperately, and whose fur was wet with his tears.

Later, when the kettle was whistling and his swollen eyes were dry, Owen went downstairs for tea. His mother asked no questions, nor did she mention the green rabbit on her son's knees. Mam could be very understanding sometimes.

At last Owen volunteered, 'Constable Wynn says it's all right, and he doesn't want you to be worried, Mam, because you're a fine woman.'

Mrs Owen sighed and said, 'He's a wonderful man, is Davy Wynn, and don't you forget it!'

They all looked at her in surprise. She had never called anyone but their dad, a wonderful man.

The Storm

The village eventually forgave Owen-Owen. They decided that Mrs Owen's eldest boy had 'gone off the rails' temporarily, because of missing his dad. Mrs Price was an exception. She refused to speak to Owen and referred to him as 'that wicked boy' for a long time afterwards.

Elin and Owen did not discuss Tatty Apple's bad behaviour for several days, but one evening, feeling rather cross, Elin followed her brother into the garden and accused him of keeping a thoroughly bad rabbit.

'He's just bad, through and through,' she told Owen.

'He's not bad,' cried Owen. 'Not all bad.'

'Have you ever seen him do anything good?' asked Elin.

Owen thought for several seconds; at last he replied, 'He makes us laugh and he hasn't had a chance to do anything really good yet. I'm sure he's only bad when he's angry. Being left in the guinea-pig cage, he didn't like that so he moved the mirror and things; going shopping, he hated that so he stole the chocolates, and when you called him a silly old rabbit, he was furious so he threw your bed about.'

'He can't do anything good, anything noble!' scoffed Elin.

Her brother jumped to his feet. 'Noble is the word,' he cried. 'Tatty Apple is a noble rabbit and one day he will prove it. At least he does SOMETHING, your chicken doesn't do anything, she can't even lay an egg!'

This was a sore point with Elin, who immediately burst into tears.

'I'm sorry, Elin,' said Owen. 'I shouldn't have said that.'

'She's so sad,' sobbed his sister. 'You never take any notice of her, nobody does, except me. I bet you haven't looked at her for a week.'

'I s'pose I haven't,' agreed Owen.

He went over to Poppy and took a good long look at her. He was quite shocked. Poppy sat on her perch with her head down; her once shining feathers were dull and drooping and she had even lost part of her lovely black tail.

'She needs cheering up,' said Owen. 'Let's take her down to the river.'

'What for?' asked Elin.

'It'll make her feel better – come on!'

Elin shook her head, nevertheless she accompanied her brother down to the river, carrying a large plastic bag full of Poppy. Owen carried a bag containing Tatty Apple.

When they reached the river bank they put the rabbit and the chicken side by side at the edge of the water. Tatty Apple immediately scuttled away into the nettles. Poppy stared at her reflection; this seemed to depress her even more; she turned away from the bedraggled chicken in the water, sat down and closed her eyes.

'Oh dear,' said Elin.

Suddenly a shower of grass and leaves gathered together in a bright blanket and fell softly on Poppy, covering every part of her. For a moment Poppy vanished, but when, at last, her head emerged through the patchwork of leaves, a garland of flowers fell from nowhere and settled at a jaunty angle on her red comb.

'Queen Poppy,' cried Elin. 'With a cloak of leaves and a crown of flowers. Look, O-O! Clever old Tatty Apple has made her better, she's all bright and fluffy. Poppy's happy again.'

'Perhaps she'll lay an egg,' said Owen.

'I hope so,' Elin sighed. 'It'll be such a beautiful first egg, I know.' And it was.

It was late when the children left the woods and, as they ran beside the shining river, singing all the songs they could remember, a shadow moved behind them.

Mostyn Mathias had followed Elin and Owen every time they visited the river. He had seen Tatty Apple's magic and he was afraid of it. He did not want to believe the strange things that he had seen, and he determined to put a stop to them as soon as he had an opportunity.

Spring passed. The gentle bluebells and primroses died. The woods beside the river were filled with new leaves, thick weeds and the strong, sweet smell of cow parsley and elderflowers. The school term ended and Elin and Owen could spend all their days with Poppy and Tatty Apple. Every day since her visit to the river bank Poppy had laid a large brown egg in her nesting-box. And Tatty Apple's magic became even more marvellous. One day he lifted a branch, half as big as a tree, and rode it through the woods.

It was about this time that Mrs Owen started her night work. She had always made clothes for the children on her old sewing machine, but one day a new sewing machine arrived. It was twice the size of the other; it had more knobs, levers, spare reels and needles than Tom could count. With her new sewing machine Mrs Owen began to make clothes for Other People. Jackets, trousers, skirts, baby clothes; she made anything for anybody. She worked all the evening, all the night, and sometimes almost until dawn. Elin and Owen, Tom and Huwie became accustomed to the humming and clicking of their mother's new night-time occupation and learned to sleep through it. But Owen could not look into her tired, red eyes in the morning without feeling sad and a little ashamed. All the new toys, the new clothes and extra cakes on Saturday, could not make up for Mam's smiling morning face, which, now, they rarely saw.

One afternoon Mrs Owen called Elin into the kitchen and gave her two five-pound notes. 'It's to take Tom and Owen-Owen on the train,' she explained. 'I've got so much work to do, Elin, I'll have to be at the machine all afternoon. Mrs Morris will take Huwie for a few hours, but I want you to take the others on the train, both ways, twice. Take your anoraks, buy them sweets and crisps, whatever you want. I've a wedding dress to make, see, and I dare not do it wrong and spoil the lovely material.'

Elin could hardly believe she had so much money to spend. 'Can I see it, Mam?' was all she could say. 'Can I see the lovely material?'

Mrs Owen smiled. 'You can have a look,' she said. 'But don't touch!'

Elin peeped into the sitting-room. There was a sheet of brown paper on the table, and, on the brown paper, a roll of white, silky stuff. She went into the room, closed the door behind her, and crept over to the table. The wedding dress would be more beautiful than anything the village had ever seen, she thought. It would be a princess's dress, with a white frill at the neck, and long, wide sleeves. No. It would not have frills, it would be tight, tight, the sleeves like silken skin. She looked at her hands; they were quite clean; very gently, she took a corner of the material between her thumb and forefinger.

'It's like a fairy's wing,' Elm murmured.

'What is?' Tom had come into the room and was about to leap forward, but Elin ran to him, heaved him through the door and slammed it shut.

'It's nothing,' she said. 'Mam's work. You're not to go in there. You're coming on the train with us. Let's go and tell O-O.'

'I'm going to take Tatty Apple,' Owen said, when he heard the good news. 'We'll be out all afternoon.'

'You can't take him on a train,' grumbled his sister. 'You'll have to get a special ticket or something.'

'Not if he's in a bag,' said Owen.

Elin sighed, 'Go on, hurry up and get him, then.'

While Owen was arranging Tatty Apple comfortably within the carrier-bag, Elin smoothed Tom's hair, rubbed the orange juice off his chin with her handkerchief and zipped up his anorak.

Tom was still chattering with excitement when they began to run down the hill. By the time they had reached the station, however, he had barely enough energy to hop, and none at all for speech.

Elin bought three tickets, a giant bag of crisps, three bars of chocolate and a packet of fruit pastilles. Then, looking round at the boys' eager faces, she bought a roll of peppermints, just in case.

They decided to stay in the carriage this time. Tom would have been happy anywhere. Jo Briggs, the driver, was still on the platform talking to Mr Evans, the stationmaster. Jo seemed anxious, he kept looking along the track towards the river. Mr Evans pointed to the ticket office, he threw out his arm indicating the passengers peering from the train windows.

'Just this one, Jo,' said the stationmaster. 'We'll cancel the next run if the weather gets any worse.'

Jo shook his head. 'I don't like the look of that river,' he muttered, then he climbed aboard.

As the train began to roll out of the station a distant roll of thunder coincided with a hiss of steam from the engine. Owen looked out of the window. The sky above Llanibont had been clear and blue a few moments ago, but as they moved away a giant black cloud climbed out of the hills and swept over the village, hiding it from the sun.

'There's the river,' yelled Tom. 'I can see a fish. Look! Look! It's very high, the river; right to the top of the bank.'

So that was why Jo had been looking at the river. What if the black cloud brought more rain? Perhaps it was already raining up-country. The water would be running off the hills and filling the river. They knew all about rain in Llanibont. Still they were quite safe on the train, Elin thought.

At that moment a light flurry of raindrops pattered against the windowpane. The black cloud was right above them.

'It's gone very dark,' said Owen. 'The river's higher than I've ever seen it. It wasn't like that when we came down. It must be rising very fast.'

'The train will be all right,' Elin said, more to reassure herself than to calm her brother.

The pattering raindrops became a drumbeat, thudding upon the train, and all along the carriage passengers thrust their windows up with a bang, as the rain spattered in upon hands and faces.

Castell Coch looked deep purple under the heavy sky, and when they reached the mill, water was lapping at the doors.

They entered the tunnel and all was quiet for a while, but no sooner had they emerged into the rain again, when there was a screech of brakes and the wheels of the little train whined to a halt.

They sat in their seats listening to the huff-puff of the engine and the beating of the rain, until one of the passengers, a big man with a curly moustache, jumped up and strode to the end of the carriage and out on to the balcony. He was back in a second.

'It's a ruddy great tree,' he shouted to his fellow passengers. 'Fallen on to the track. It'll take a lot of shifting.'

The big man's wife gave a little scream and several people pulled down their windows, thrusting their heads out into the rain. There were exclamations of horror and an elderly woman began to hiccup.

Owen pulled down his window.

'Can you see the tree, O-O?' asked Elin.

'Yes, and I can see the river too, it's almost up to the track,' said Owen.

Jo Briggs suddenly popped his head in at the end of the carriage. 'Gentlemen,' he shouted. 'We need help with a tree up front, can some of you lend a hand?'

Every man in the carriage jumped to his feet and leapt through the door at the end. Owen was about to follow them when Elin caught the back of his anorak. 'Don't be silly, O-O. You're not big enough! You'll fall in the river and no one will see you.'

Her brother struggled briefly and then saw the debris whirling along on waves that lashed across the river. He sank back on to his seat and pulled Tatty Apple's bag closer to him.

Men began to run past the windows back into the tunnel. Women and children gradually fell silent, and still the little engine puff-puffed into the storm, ready to go whenever it was able.

After some time the men began to file back into the carriage, shaking water and mud from their hair, their hands, their clothes and their shoes.

'Can't you shift it, Bill?' asked the big man's wife.

Bill shook his head.

'I suppose we'll have to go back then,' said his wife.

'Can't do that, May! Tunnel's full of water!' Bill was breathing heavily.

Elin shivered and an ice-cold lump turned in her stomach. Tom flung his arms round her and pressed his face into her lap. She smiled, rather weakly, at Owen, and Owen sat very stiff and still, holding the rabbit in its bag, close to his chest.

Suddenly everyone in the carriage began to talk; children cried; someone coughed and coughed. The noise subsided then started up again. They were talking about ropes, about climbing over the tree, about falling into the river. There were people on the train who could climb over the tree, but there were some who could not. The old lady hiccupping, and some of the children could not.

On the other side of the train a steep bank rose, almost sheer, about fifty feet until it reached a narrow sheep track that wound round the hill. There was no escape that way.

Tom began to cry and Elin held him tighter. Owen stood up and looked out of the window. The river was washing against the wheels of the train. Still holding Tatty

Apple close to him, he began to walk along the carriage towards the engine.

'O-O, where are you going?' squeaked Elin.

'Just to see,' said Owen.

'Don't go, O-O! Stay here!' begged Elin.

'I won't be long, I just want to see,' replied her brother.

He felt very strange. He was uncertain of what he was about to attempt, but it had something to do with Tatty Apple and the tree. Owen stepped out of the door on to the balcony. He could see the tree through the dark haze of smoke pouring out of the engine's funnel. The tree looked even bigger now that he was close to it; black and shiny like a serpent.

Slowly Owen lifted Tatty Apple up to his

shoulder, letting the bag drop to the floor. The rabbit blinked one dark green eye and regarded the smoke and the black tree.

'Remember the branch, Tatty Apple?' Owen asked softly. 'The tree is bigger, but can you do it? I wouldn't ask but there doesn't seem to be any other way, and I think somebody is going to be hurt soon, Tom or Elin, or even me.'

He stroked the rabbit's nose very gently, very slowly, over and over again. Tatty Apple closed his eyes. 'Can you move the tree?' Owen whispered. 'Please?'

The green rabbit quivered and pressed his nose into the boy's arm. Owen stared out at the black tree, huge and motionless.

'Come inside, O-O!' Elin was pulling at him. 'You've been out here for ages. What are you doing? You're soaked.'

Owen stepped back into the carriage and allowed Elin to lead him back to his seat.

'What's the matter with Tatty Apple?' Elin asked.

The green rabbit had slumped, almost lifeless on to Owen's lap, his eyes were closed and his ears lay flat against his body.

'He's been thinking,' said Owen.

Elin looked hard at her brother and began to bite her lip. 'He couldn't do . . . that,' she whispered, and Owen knew that she understood what he had been trying to do. He shrugged and stroked the rabbit's ears.

'I'm not waiting!' Bill jumped up violently, pulling his wife to her feet. 'We'll try the tunnel,' he said. 'Is anyone coming with us?'

'There could be three feet of water in there, by now,' someone said. 'And the current will be vicious.'

'It's worth a try,' Bill roared. Then he looked at Tom and Elin. 'Might be a bit deep for children, but I could carry the little one.'

Owen looked up at the big man. 'The tree will move,' he said.

Bill smiled. 'No, son, I'm sorry, it'll need a crane to shift that thing.'

'It'll move,' said Owen.

Bill laughed sheepishly.

'Well,' he said, 'we're trying for the tunnel.'
Before he could reach the other end of the
carriage there was a loud toot-toot from the
engine. Everyone rushed to the windows.

They heard a grinding, grumbling
groan, and the train began to shake as the
giant tree rolled sideways and sank slowly
into the swollen river.

Nobody cheered, though they felt they
should have. Everyone was so relieved, so
thankful and amazed. They sank back into
their seats and began to chatter, a few to
giggle.

The train climbed the hill that took
them away from the river and through a
field bright with buttercups. Even in the
rain, at the sight of all that gold, everyone
had to smile. And then, far away, they saw
the great black tree bobbing on the flood.

'Look at the tree, O-O,' said Elin. 'It doesn't seem so big now, does it?'

But Owen could not look at the tree. Tatty Apple lay cool and still beside him: he was not even sure if the little rabbit's heart was beating.

The Catapult

When the train finally pulled into
Llyndu station, the narrow platform
was crowded with onlookers, ambulance-
men and police.

As the passengers alighted from the
train, some silent, some chattering
nervously, they were surrounded by groups
of friends and relatives.

Owen tucked Tatty Apple under his
anorak, so that no one should see the
rabbit. He wished Mam had been there, but

she did not have a car. There was no one to take them home.

'What shall we do, Elin?' Owen asked.

'I don't know,' his sister replied.

They looked at each other feeling rather lost, but trying not to let Tom know it. And then, suddenly Owen felt a heavy hand on his shoulder and a deep voice above him said, 'Come on, children. I'm taking you back to Mam,' and Davy Wynn put one arm round Owen, and the other round Tom and Elin, and shepherded them towards his police car.

Owen had not felt so happy to see anyone, since his dad's last visit. But on the way home in Davy Wynn's car, he could find nothing to say. No one made a sound except Tom, chewing the forgotten crisps and chocolate.

When they got home Mrs Owen was waiting in the open door with Huwie in her arms. News travelled fast in Llanibont but Mam had guessed the trouble even before Mrs Price had tapped on her door and shouted, 'The river's in flood, Beti. And the train's stuck on the line. Your children are on it, I believe. I heard it from Ifor Pugh, he can see it from his farm.'

Now the children were home again, and, trying to embrace them all at the same

time, she drew them into the kitchen and plied them with hot cocoa, bread and marmite and raspberry buns.

Davy Wynn went quietly away, leaving the children alone with their mother. She gazed intently at their flushed faces as they chewed and chattered. 'Well, what happened then?' she asked at last. 'Did the men move the tree, or what?'

'The men didn't do nothing,' said Owen. 'The tree moved by itself.'

'But someone must have . . .' Mrs Owen stopped. Owen had sprung to his feet with Tatty Apple still clasped in his arms.

'I said it just moved, didn't I?' shouted Owen. 'Well, it did, it just moved!'

'I see,' said Mrs Owen softly. 'Owen-Owen, what's wrong with your rabbit? Is he ill?'

'I don't know, Mam,' Owen's voice began to shake. 'I don't know. He's . . . he's just been thinking too much. I'm going to take him to bed.'

Mrs Owen did not interfere. Later, when she went to straighten Tom's and Huwie's blankets, she found her eldest son fast asleep with Tatty Apple out-stretched beneath his bed.

In the middle of the night the rain stopped and by dawn there was a strong breeze and a golden sky. Owen awoke as the sun rose. Tatty Apple was lying in exactly the same position as he had left him. Owen picked up the rabbit and laid him on the bed, then he dressed hurriedly and carried Tatty Apple down into the garden.

Poppy was making a great fuss in her

tiny hen-coop, so Owen lifted the latch on her door and she came running out for breakfast.

'Sorry, Poppy, it's only me,' said Owen. 'Elin will bring your corn later.'

He put Tatty Apple beside the red hen and the little rabbit opened his green eyes and pricked up his ears. He began to pant very fast, and his small head jerked up and down in time with his breathing.

'What is it, Tatty Apple? What have I done?' Owen cried. 'Was it too much, what I asked you to do yesterday? Has it hurt you, all that . . . thinking?'

He picked up the green rabbit and held him close. As he did so, he heard a low chuckling sound behind him and a voice said, 'Sick is he?' He turned to see Mostyn Mathias leaning over the garden wall.

'I been watching you, Owen-Owen,'
said Mostyn darkly. 'You and that rabbit.
He's peculiar, isn't he? I seen you in the

woods. I'm gonna get your rabbit, I am!'
And he held up his catapult. 'Better than a
gun this is! It'll be easy 'cos he can't run
now, can he?'

Owen held Tatty Apple tightly. 'Go
away, Mostyn Mathias!' he yelled.

Mostyn's grinning white face slowly

disappeared behind the wall and Owen rushed indoors.

Mrs Owen was in a particularly happy mood that morning. After the anxiety of the day before, she would have allowed her children to do almost anything. Owen fed Tatty Apple crusts and cabbage leaves on the kitchen floor, but Tatty Apple had little appetite.

After lunch Mam went back to her sewing machine: Elin, Tom and Huwie went into the back garden. Owen wanted to leave the house but something made him too afraid to do so. He paced up and down the bedroom with Tatty Apple in his arms. Then, glancing out of the window, he saw Mostyn Mathias and two other boys, bigger than Mostyn, leaning against the front gate.

Owen went downstairs, opened the

front door, just an inch, and peeped through. Mostyn and his companions had moved further up the street. They were murmuring earnestly and Mostyn was waving his shiny catapult.

Owen pushed the door further open and then, suddenly, he was running. He unlatched the gate, flung it back and ran across the road. He could feel Mostyn's eyes upon him and heard three shouts as he ran up the path into the hills. He did not know why he had not stayed inside the house. But now he knew he must run for Tatty Apple's life.

The other boys' legs were longer than Owen's. They were gaining on him. He left the path and struck off, up through the middle of the field, towards the sun.

It was hot now, even in the shadow of

the hill. Owen stopped to get his breath and looked back. Mostyn and his friends had seen him, how could they have failed to see him, alone in an empty field. Owen turned and began to race up to the brow of the hill, but long before he reached it he found his feet could only stumble through the sharp stubble.

When he got to the top of the hill at last, he came face to face with the sun. The golden field before him stretched for a hundred yards then fell sharply into a rocky, wooded hillside. Owen was on one of the highest fields for miles. Around and beneath him, the green and gold patchwork of lower farms spun like a kaleidoscope, as he turned and turned and turned, not knowing which way to go. And then he saw Mostyn on the brow of the hill.

Owen raised Tatty Apple up to his face. 'You'll have to run for it now,' he whispered, and flung the rabbit, as far as he could, across the field.

For a moment Tatty Apple was still; then he sat up, on his hind legs, and looked at Owen.

'Go! Go! Go!' screamed the boy. 'Run, Tatty Apple! Run! Run! Run!'

Mostyn raised his catapult and closed

one eye. A round stone spun silently past
Owen's head, and Tatty Apple sank into the
corn. A terrible scream filled the air, and
Owen could not tell whether it came from
within him, or from the little green rabbit.
He raced wildly towards the place where
the rabbit had been, but could see nothing.

Mostyn and his friends turned away.
Owen could hear them laughing as they
wandered back to the village.

He searched every inch of the high sunlit field until his eyes ached with the hard bright emptiness of it. Then he walked wearily down into the woods, and fell asleep.

He woke before dawn and went up to the field again. It was very different now; one star remained, and the waning moon. The cut corn was pale grey and lifeless. Owen wandered slowly over the field and down the hill to the path. He could see the village below him, a cluster of tiny houses scattered beside a narrow street. There appeared to be a white van outside the Owen's house, and, as he drew nearer, he saw that it was an ambulance. He began to run down the path, but before he reached the road, the ambulance drove away, its siren screeching through the dawn.

Owen ran across the road and pounded upon his front door. It was opened, a few seconds later, by Elin. Elin with a red tearstained face.

'Where have you been, O-O?' sobbed Elin. 'Mam was in such a state. She fell down the stairs, O-O! An' I rang 999, an' Davy Wynn came, an' the ambulance came, an' they've taken her away, O-O! She wasn't saying nothing an' she was white, white as . . . white-as-the-wedding-dress-on-her-sewing-machine!'

There was a policewoman inside the house. A plump, cheerful person called Enid. She gave the children their breakfast, helped them to dress, and kept them busy with games, with eating, with washing and with stories, till suppertime.

Owen did not tell Elin about Tatty

Apple. He did not know how to. He could hardly bring himself to think of the green rabbit and what had happened on the high field. He pushed the memory of it to the back of his mind while he thought of Mam.

'Your mam's going to be all right,' said Enid, when she tucked the boys into bed that night. 'But someone nice will come and look after you until she's quite better.'

Dreadful Mrs Drain

Mrs Drain was not nice. The children hated her on sight. Mrs Drain was from Social Services. She had wanted to look after someone old and quiet, but they had got her name muddled up at the office, and now here she was and not liking it one bit.

Mrs Drain smelled of boiled cabbage and sour milk. She was not fat and she was not thin; she was no shape at all. Her clothes were not coloured and nor was her hair. She liked dumplings, bread pudding and privacy. She did not like noise or mess or sunlight; she did not like children either. But she would have done anything for the money.

When Mrs Drain arrived Tom screamed, 'Go away!' Huwie threw his shoe at her and Owen hid under the kitchen table.

'The boys are very upset,' Enid explained. 'But Elin's a good girl, she'll be a great help, I'm sure.' And away went cheerful Enid.

'Come back! Come back!' Tom screamed through the kitchen window. 'I don't like Mrs Drain.'

'Ta-ra, boys!' called Enid happily. She got into her smart little car and away she went down the hill, taking all her cheerfulness with her.

There began the worst week the children could ever remember. Every day seemed to be filled with chores. With washing and scrubbing, with making beds, drying, tidying, dusting, sweeping and weeding. There was never a minute of peace with Mrs Drain. The face flannels were always boiling, cabbages were always boiling and so was Huwie's bottle: the house was full of steam and disinfectant. It became, in Tom's words, 'A really nasty house.'

A few days after Mrs Owen's accident, Davy Wynn took the children to see her in the hospital at Llyndu. Mam was very pale, her eyes looked huge and black and though she hugged them as tight as she was able, the children felt only a light warm touch.

'Mam's tired,' said Davy Wynn. 'Let her rest now, and we'll come another day.'

Davy Wynn had never talked about the night Mam fell down the stairs; never asked Owen where he had been; never blamed him. Owen was very grateful for that.

On the way home the big policeman told the children that their mother had been working too hard. 'She's been lonely too, without your dad, but we're going to take care of her when she's better, aren't we, children?'

'Yes,' they agreed, and did not think it strange that Davy Wynn had said 'we'.

Mrs Drain's second week was worse than her first. She had begun to get bad-tempered as well as mean and fussy. Now it was 'early to bed', 'bread without jam', and 'silence at meals'.

Poor Huwie got the worst of it. He couldn't help spilling things, falling over or getting dirty. Mam had understood, Mrs Drain did not.

Huwie cried a great deal during Mrs Drain's first week and then he stopped; he stopped eating and he stopped trying to talk. When Enid paid them a quick visit one day, Owen blurted out, 'Huwie's ill, Enid.'

'Nonsense, he's fine!' Mrs Drain glared at Owen. She picked Huwie up, gave him a horrid sort of hug and pecked at his cheek.

'He's lovely little boy,' said Enid. 'And you've all been so lucky to have Mrs Drain to look after you. Being so little, I expect Huwie still misses his mam.'

'Very much!' said Owen dramatically. 'Very, very much!'

'Well, I'd better be popping along now,' said Enid. 'It's been lovely to see you all, be good children. Ta-ra!'

The door slammed and the house was cold again.

'We'll have to go,' Owen told Elin. He had sneaked into her room after dark. 'No one understands. Huwie might be dead before Mam gets back.'

'Don't be silly,' Elin whispered. 'It won't be long now. Anyway where would we go?'

'To Mam,' said Owen.

'That wouldn't be fair. She's ill, she needs a rest. You know what Davy Wynn said.'

Owen thought about Davy Wynn. He thought about the time when Tatty Apple had played tricks in the village. He remembered Davy Wynn in the sitting-room, telling him to come and have a chat if he felt a bit down. But Tatty Apple was gone. How could Davy Wynn help?

'Tatty Apple is dead!' Owen said abruptly.

Elin looked at him in disbelief. 'How?' she asked at last.

'Mostyn Mathias shot him with his catapult.'

Elin gasped. 'Are you sure?'

'He fell down and he screamed and he never came to me when I called. But I couldn't find his body.'

'Perhaps he is afraid, and is hiding,' Elin suggested. 'Why don't you go to Ty Uchaf? That's where he came from.'

'Ty Uchaf?' Owen thought of strange Mr Evans and his dark farmhouse in the hills. 'No. Let's go to Mam, Elin?'

'Davy Wynn said Mam must rest and not worry,' replied his sister. 'We can't run away, O-O!'

'All right. But I think Huwie will die,' Owen muttered, and he slammed Elin's door.

He thought about Elin's suggestion, however, and throughout the following day he kept remembering that cold spring evening, when the green rabbit had appeared out of the wind. After tea he slipped out of the house. Mrs Drain was throwing saucepans into the kitchen cupboard, and did not hear the front door 'click' behind him.

It was a fine warm evening, and the climb to Ty Uchaf did not seem as steep as it had before. But as soon as he reached the top of the stony path, a wind sprang up from nowhere. A strange, icy wind that seemed to whisper round his head.

There was no sign of Mr Evans in the farmyard, but a muddy blue tractor was parked beside the back door.

'Mr Evans!' Owen called. 'It's me, Owen-Owen. Do you remember me, Mr Evans? I came about the hen?'

There was a movement behind one of the dark windows. He was sure Mr Evans was in the house.

'I found a rabbit here, Mr Evans. A green rabbit; a special rabbit. But now I've lost him . . . Did he come back here, Mr Evans?'

Owen waited for an answer but the farmhouse was as silent as a stone.

'Can you hear me, Mr Evans?' cried Owen. 'I need to know about the rabbit.'

If Mr Evans was in the house, nothing was going to bring him out, nothing was going to make him reply.

'Where is Tatty Apple?' Owen screamed at the dark window. 'Is he here? Who is going to tell me?'

He might as well have asked the wind.

He stumbled down the path from Ty Uchaf, pausing in the oak grove where he had picked bluebells for Mam, so many weeks ago. There were tall purple foxgloves there now, but Mam was not at home and he had no wish to take flowers to Mrs Drain.

When he reached Llanibont he had tears in his eyes and he almost walked into Mostyn Mathias. Owen sprang away from the older boy and glared at him.

'Hullo, Owen-Owen,' said Mostyn quietly. 'I been looking for you.'

'What d'you want me for?' growled
Owen.

'I got something for you,' Mostyn
sounded almost timid.

'I don't want nothing from you,' said
Owen.

'Please! It's to make up, like . . . for the
rabbit.' Mostyn put his hand into his pocket
and drew out a large bar of chocolate
which he tentatively held out to Owen.

Owen stared at the chocolate, then he suddenly grabbed it, threw it to the ground and brought the tip of his heel down upon it, again and again and again.

The red and gold paper split and tiny grains of brown chocolate burst out and spattered the pavement. 'Nothing can make up for my rabbit,' he said. He kicked the remaining tiny bits of gold paper towards Mostyn and ran up to the house.

The door was open and Mrs Drain was waiting for him. Owen did not protest when he was sent to bed without his supper. By the smell coming from the kitchen he knew it was something really nasty. When Elin passed his door on her way to bed, however, he could not help calling out, 'Let's go to Mam, Elin?'

'Not yet, O-O,' whispered Elin. 'I'm

sorry about the supper, but we can't go yet.'

The following day Elin changed her mind. Poppy had not laid an egg for a week, and this was irritating Mrs Drain.

'I think we'll have to get her some more grit, Mrs Drain,' Elin said. 'And some more chicken food, and she doesn't get scraps like she used to, because you make us eat everything.'

'That hen is old,' said Mrs Drain. 'Scraps, grit, it's all nonsense. She's old. She'll have to go in the pot!'

'In the pot?' Elin was aghast.

'In the pot. The oven, child! That hen is finished!'

Elin opened her mouth very wide and screamed at Mrs Drain. Still screaming, she ran into the garden, grabbed Poppy and carried her up to her room. She did not emerge for lunch, nor tea, and when Mrs Drain finally tried to force her way in, Elin informed her that Mam had provided her with a key and they would have to bash the door in before they got her red hen.

Mrs Drain came downstairs very slowly. Her lips were tight and her eyes hard. 'You can go to bed now, boys,' she said.

Tom and Owen got down obediently. Huwie remained in his seat. Owen lifted him out of his highchair and set him on the floor, but Huwie's legs crumpled under him and he lay spread-eagled on the mat.

'I don't think he can walk, Mrs Drain,' Owen said.

'Can't walk, is it?' shouted the exasperated Mrs Drain. 'Can't talk, can't eat! It's WON'T talk, WON'T walk, WON'T eat, more like!'

'Don't shout, Mrs Drain,' Owen pleaded. 'Please, don't. It hurts him.'

Owen pulled Huwie to his feet and, with Tom's help, managed to get the little boy up the stairs to the bedroom.

It was evident that Mrs Drain wanted nothing more to do with them that night, so Tom and Owen washed Huwie, took off his clothes, pulled on his pyjamas, and put him in his cot.

Owen was so tired he lay on his bed and fell asleep still fully dressed.

He awoke with a start. It was still dark but there was something tall and pale at the foot of his bed: Elin, dressed in her yellow anorak and pale blue skirt. Poppy was tucked beneath her arm.

'What are you doing, Elin? Is it morning?' Owen rubbed his eyes.

'It's night,' hissed Elin. 'We're going. Now.'

'Now?' Owen sat up. 'But it's so dark, Elin, and Huwie's ill. How can we go?'

'We must go,' Elin whispered. 'Hold Poppy.' She put the red hen firmly into her brother's arms, then she strode over to Tom's bed and shook him awake.

'Get dressed quickly, Tom,' Elin said quietly. 'Put on your shirt, your trousers and your shoes, and get your anorak. We're going.'

Tom swung his legs over the side of his bed and yawned. He pulled off his pyjama top and felt for the muddle of clothes on the chair beside him.

Elin opened the curtains and the room was filled with the soft light of the moon. She bent over Huwie's cot and gently wrapped his blankets round him. Then she lifted him on to her shoulder, just as she had seen Mam do, and carried him out of the room.

With one arm holding Poppy firmly to his chest, Owen helped Tom to do his buttons, his shoelaces and the zip of his anorak. Then he took his brother's hand

and followed Elin. Tom did not say a word until the little procession had reached the bottom of the stairs. 'Why is it so dark?' he asked in a loud voice.

'Sssssshhhh!' hissed Elin. 'It's night and we're going to Mam, and we don't want to wake Mrs Drain.' She lifted the latch and they crept out into the cool night air.

The High Field

The door clicked shut behind them and Owen drew a deep breath. There was no going back now. Hand in hand he and Tom walked to the gate, flung it open and then ran across the road. There was no doubt in Owen's mind that they would travel through the woods and fields rather than on the road.

Elin and the sleeping Huwie followed more slowly. Already her brother had begun to weigh heavily in her arms, but she

carried him up the path without a moan
until they reached the bridge over the river
and there, at last, she had to lay him on the
ground, while she rubbed her aching
shoulders.

Huwie awoke and began to sob. He
turned in his blankets and saw the silver
moonlight on the river; for a moment he
stopped crying and gazed at the water.

'Can you walk, Huwie?' Elin asked.
'We're going to see Mam. If you could walk
it would help so much.'

Huwie did not seem to hear her.

'It's going to take a long time to get him
to Llyndu,' said Tom.

'If only he would walk, just a bit,' said
Elin helplessly.

'I'll carry him.' Owen thrust Poppy at
his sister and gathered the crumpled mass

of blankets into his arms. Then he flung
Huwie over his shoulder and began to run
up the hill, away from the path.

'Where are you going?' cried Elin. 'Are
you mad, O-O?'

Owen kept going; stumbling over the
stubble towards the high field where
Mostyn Mathias's grey stone had spun
through the air, and Tatty Apple had fallen
into the corn.

As Owen climbed the steep hill,
Huwie's body dragged upon his arms as
though it would tear them from him, but he
plodded on, upwards and upwards until he
reached the brow of the hill, and there he
sat his brother down, with the pattern of
moonlit fields, of trees and moving grey
sheep beneath and around him.

Huwie frowned up at the stars and then

looked at Owen. Owen did not know why he had brought Huwie to the empty field. He gazed at the place where the green rabbit had fallen, only two weeks ago.

Suddenly Huwie tugged Owen's sleeve, 'Look, Owen-Owen,' he said urgently. 'Look, rabbit!'

At first Owen could see nothing, but Huwie was pulling himself up to lean against his brother; now he began to walk hesitantly away from Owen towards something moving across the field.

There were plenty of rabbits hiding in the hedgerows at that time of year, but Owen knew that the rabbit Huwie could see had eyes as green as the reflection of leaves in a river. Tatty Apple had not died. He had been hiding away from them all until his strength returned. Waiting, perhaps, for the right moment to show himself.

Huwie was leaping through the stubble now, and so was the rabbit. Huwie began to laugh. 'Look, look!' he giggled. 'Owen-Owen, Tom, Elin. Look, green rabbit!'

Tom and Elin had reached the field. They ran to Owen and watched Huwie and the rabbit.

Then Tatty Apple vanished and, for a moment, Huwie stood alone in the middle of the field, turning, turning, and called to the rabbit.

The wild grass beside the headgerow began to sway and a shower of bright poppies sailed into the sky, blue cornflowers followed them, and from the fallow field beyond, sprays of white and gold daisies came tumbling and twirling; purple

campion and tiny blue harebells blew from
the woods, and gathering together, the
rainbow of wild flowers spun round
Huwie's head, rustling like water over the
river stones.

Huwie leapt up to touch the colours.
The rainbow fled away and Huwie
followed, jumping over the ground in bare
feet and blue striped pyjamas.

Owen could not help but follow his
brother, jumping up to touch the flowers as
Huwie did, and nearly catching one. He
could hear Tom and Elin rushing after him
and saw Poppy fly past and take a
cornflower in her beak. Owen laughed,
Tom laughed and Elin sang, and then she
began to dance. Tom became an aeroplane,
arms outstretched and zooming round the

field; Huwie was a bird, flapping and bouncing; Owen, the engine, elbows stiff and bent, 'Chuff! Chuff! Chuff!' he went. They raced round the field in ever widening circles until Elin sank breathless to the ground, and the singing stopped.

The boys stood still and watched the flowers climbing higher and higher; they whirled round the field once more, in strange and beautiful patterns, and then they formed a bright stream that swept away to the river. A dark shape chased the flowers down the hill – Tatty Apple following his magic.

Owen knew then that the green rabbit would never return to them. But he also knew that they would always be able to find Tatty Apple, up here in the high woods and fields, when they needed him most.

When the last flower had disappeared the children crept under a hedge and, huddled together in Huwie's blankets, they slept. Before birdsong had begun to fill the valleys, the little family arose, stretched themselves and silently filed down the hill. Huwie led them, smiling at the dew on his bare feet, his red blanket round his shoulders like a prince's cloak.

Elin found Poppy scratching for seeds beneath a hedge. She tucked the hen into her anorak and Poppy snuggled down, hoping for a better breakfast elsewhere.

They decided that the quickest way to reach Llyndu was to walk all the way along the railway track. Not one of them felt tired after the night's adventure, and they reached the town before the milkman had started his rounds. Only a few inquisitive heads peered out of windows, to mutter at the strange little procession marching up to the cottage hospital.

Elin rang the hospital bell and pushed open the door. The children shuffled into a hall with a clean shiny floor and a smell of Mrs Drain about it. A big woman, rustling in a tight blue dress, appeared. She did not ask the children their names, she merely raised her eyebrows and pulled them, one by one, into a room.

'Here they are!' she said.

Davy Wynn got up from a chair and stared at them. He looked bigger than ever. The children stared back, a little apprehensive, but happy too, now that they had reached their destination.

Davy Wynn shook his head. 'Well, it's bad children, you are,' he said solemnly.

'You know, I suppose, that I've been looking for you these past hours. What have you got to say for yourselves, eh?' He folded his arms across his chest and waited.

'How's Mam?' asked Owen.

'She's just fine,' said the policeman. 'We didn't tell her about your little escapade. No need to worry her when I guessed all along that you'd turn up here, like bad pennies the lot of you.'

'We want to see our mam,' Elin demanded.

Davy Wynn frowned. 'When she wakes,' he said. 'But only for a minute or two, and you're not to go worrying her with your tales of woe.'

Suddenly the big policeman bent down and lifted Huwie on to his shoulder. 'Before you go in to see your mam, children,' he said, 'there's something I have to tell you. It could be a good thing for you . . . er, depending on how you look at it.' He began to pace up and down the room.

'Look at what?' asked Tom.

'Well . . . the situation.' Davy Wynn's complexion became a shade redder than usual.

Owen had the impression that, for once, the big policeman needed help. 'Is it about Mrs Drain?' he suggested.

Davy Wynn ceased his pacing. He looked relieved. 'Yes, you could say it concerned that lady,' he said. 'You see, when you leave here, you're not going back to her, you're coming home with me.'

'Hooray!' shouted Tom and Owen, and Huwie clapped his hands.

Huwie was swiftly lowered to the floor.

'Poor Mrs Drain,' said Davy Wynn. 'She did her best for you. Well, after the trouble last night she's packed her bags, and she's going home. But that's not why you're coming with me, no,' he cleared his throat. 'It's because your mam has . . . has graciously agreed to be my wife.'

There was a stunned silence. The children stared at the policeman until he was compelled to move to the door. 'You'll be hungry,' he muttered. 'We'll get you some nice hot tea and toast.'

Owen was overwhelmed by such a feeling of happiness that he could not speak. He ran to Davy Wynn and pressed his face into the hard round buttons of his uniform.

Davy Wynn smiled an enormous smile. Elin could count almost every one of his big teeth.

When the children had been filled and warmed with tea and toast, they filed into the hospital ward to see their mother, who had just been woken for her breakfast.

Mrs Owen was very surprised to see her children so early in the morning.

'Davy Wynn brought us,' Elin explained.

At the mention of the policeman's name, Mrs Owen seemed to relax. She hugged and kissed her three older children and last of all Huwie. 'Little Huwie,' she murmured. 'There are leaves in your hair. Have you been to the wood so early, and in your pyjamas too?'

There was a sudden diversion. Poppy poked her head out of Elin's anorak and cackled very loudly.

'Oh dear,' said Mam. 'Why is Poppy here?'

'Mrs Drain was going to cook her,' said Tom.

Just as Mam was beginning to look anxious Davy Wynn appeared. Mrs Owen gave him the sort of smile the children had always known as the special smile that belonged to each of them alone.

'Has . . . has Mr Wynn . . . Davy told you our news?' Mam asked.

The children looked at each other and Elin said, 'Yes, and we think you've made a very wise choice, Mam.'

'Everything's going to be all right now.' Owen took his mother's hand. 'It's going to be just great!'

'Better go now, children,' said Davy Wynn. 'Mam's getting tired.'

They kissed their mother again, but when Huwie's turn came he suddenly held out his clenched fist, then he slowly uncurled his fingers and revealed a tiny blue harebell, as soft and fresh as if it had been picked only a moment before.

Huwie put the flower into Mam's hand and closed her fingers tight upon it.

'From Tatty Apple!' he said.

Ill

Will,

Well

Nell

For Guilsfield Primary School, where I met Will.
J. N.

Contents

~

Contents

1. The almost-tree-house

Will and Nell Shepherd lived on a farm. Their house was built on the side of a hill and from every window they could see fields and sheep and sky.

Things happened to Will: accidents, illnesses, sick-bugs, coughs, earaches and all sorts of nasty things.

Nothing ever happened to Will's sister Nell, nothing bad that is. She was a very careful girl, always looked both ways twice before crossing the road, always wore her luminous strap and safety helmet when she was bicycling after tea, always wore her hood up on rainy days, washed her hands before meals and put sun-cream on her nose if it was very sunny.

As Will did none of these things you can imagine the sort of trouble he got into. Will

2

didn't *enjoy* being ill. He didn't *try* to get ill. He just forgot to be careful. For instance, there was the tree-house accident.

Will had always wanted a tree-house and his dad said he could have one for his birthday. Mr Shepherd chose a big sycamore tree quite close to the house. 'We can keep an eye on you there,' he told Will.

'And I can keep an eye on you,' said Will.

'Can I go in the tree-house?' asked Nell.

'Of course,' said Mr Shepherd.

'Of course *not*,' said Will. 'It's my tree-house, and you're too young. You'd do something silly.'

'I'm very careful,' Nell pointed out.

'Nell won't do any harm, I'm sure,' added Mr Shepherd.

'She's too small,' whined Will. 'She'd fall out. And, anyway, it's my birthday present, isn't it?'

Mr Shepherd shrugged and muttered, 'Yes, but presents can be shared.'

Next day, when Will and Nell came home from school, there was a rope ladder hanging from the sycamore tree. And over two wide branches that ran out from the trunk, a wide platform had been built.

'The floor of my tree-house!' Will shouted. 'Yippee!' He climbed up the ladder and began to bounce on the wooden platform.

Nell looked up at the almost-tree-house. She imagined having tea up there, with her friend Fiona. Everything would taste good in a tree-house, Nell thought, even custard which she usually hated.

4

'Come down, Will!' called Mr Shepherd. 'Those planks haven't been nailed in properly, yet. Besides, Mum says it's tea-time.'

Will climbed down the ladder which swayed as he moved. Nell watched and thought, I could do that, easy as pie.

That night it rained. The wind howled and lightning flashed across the sky. It rained all the next day as well. When Will and Nell came home from school, the tree-house hadn't been built. All the planks were still neatly stacked in the garage.

Will asked why nothing had been done and his dad said, 'Look at the rain. I can't build a tree-house in weather like this.'

'Is it going to be ready tomorrow?' Will asked.

'It depends on the weather,' said Mr Shepherd.

'But my birthday's on Saturday,' Will moaned. 'Only two days left. What am I going to tell Sam and Daniel and Wayne and . . . and Brian and Mike and Josh and Ben and Tim . . . and . . . and . . . the twins and . . .'

'Goodness,' said Mrs Shepherd. 'How many boys are coming?'

'Twelve,' said Will. 'And . . .'

'Hold on, Will, you'll never get twelve boys in the tree-house all at once,' said Mr Shepherd.

'We'll take it in turns,' said Will.

Nell thought, two girls would fit in a tree-house very nicely. If there is a tree-house.

It rained again in the night, and all the next day. When Will and Nell came home from school, Mr Shepherd looked rather solemn.

'I'm sorry, Will,' he said. 'I didn't have a chance to fix your tree-house. It's been too wet.'

'Only one day left!' cried Will. 'You promised me a tree-house for my birthday.'

Mrs Shepherd tried to change the subject. 'There's a present for you, Will.' She handed

him a small package. 'It's from Gran.'

'Can I open it, now?' asked Will.

'Save it for Saturday,' said his mum. 'And don't look so glum, Will. You can still have a party. Just tell your friends to come again when the tree-house is ready.'

'It's not the same,' Will grumbled. He didn't say a word at tea-time, he didn't even smile at Mr Shepherd's jokes.

After tea Mr Shepherd went to a meeting in the village. Will stomped off to watch TV in the sitting-room. Nell followed. After a few moments Will began to cheer up. Nell could tell that he'd had an idea. She could almost see it making its way across Will's face. Suddenly he jumped up and rubbed his hands together. 'Yes,' he murmured.

'Yes, what?' said Nell.

'I'm going out for a bit,' Will told her.

'But it's raining, you'll get wet.'

'So I'll put on my anorak and wellies.'

'Where are you going?'

Will was just about to tell Nell to mind her own business when he thought better of it. Nell might help him if he was nice to her.

'I'm going to finish the tree-house myself,' he whispered.

Nell gasped. 'You can't, you'll fall,' she whispered back.

'No I won't. You just keep Mum busy and don't you dare tell her where I am or what I'm doing. Promise?'

'Promise,' said Nell, very reluctantly. 'But be careful.'

From the window she watched her

brother running across the garden. He hadn't put his hood up and the rain was coming down in bucketfuls.

Nell shook her head, then she went to help her mum in the kitchen. Mrs Shepherd had made a big chocolate cake for Will's birthday. 'You can decorate it,' she told Nell.

Nell began to edge the cake with coloured icing. It was warm and peaceful in the kitchen, you couldn't hear the rain at all. After a while her mum said, 'It's very quiet. Where's Will?'

Nell didn't know what to say. She hated telling lies. It always made her feel hot and uncomfortable. But she'd made a promise to Will and she couldn't break it.

'He's in his room,' she said at last.

Soon it got so dark in the kitchen, Mum had to switch the light on. Thunder rolled across the hills and the wind started to howl.

Nell began to feel a little nagging pain in

the pit of her stomach. She wondered what had happened to Will.

'What is it, Nell?' asked her mum. 'You look worried.'

Did worry show that much? 'Nothing's the matter,' lied Nell.

A car drove into the yard and there were two heavy clunks in the porch: Mr Shepherd taking off his wellies. 'Where's Will?' he asked as he came into the kitchen. 'I've got something to show him.'

'He's in his . . . no he's . . .' Nell didn't know what to say. Her face was burning.

She tried again. 'I think he's . . . he's busy.'

'It doesn't matter,' said her dad. 'I'll show it to him later.'

But it did matter. The sky was so dark now, and the wind was growing stronger.

While her mum and dad were having a cup of tea, Nell crept out to the hall and quietly slipped on her wellies. Carefully, very carefully, she put on her anorak and pulled the hood over her head. Softly, very softly, she opened the back door, tiptoed out and closed it carefully behind her. Then she ran, ran, ran to the sycamore tree.

Will wasn't on the platform or the swinging rope ladder. Where was he?

'Will!' Nell called. 'Will, where are you?'

There was a moan quite close and then Nell saw Will. He was huddled on his side with a big plank lying on top of him.

'Will, what happened?' cried Nell.

'I slipped off the platform,' groaned Will, 'and the plank fell too. It hit my head, and my legs hurt when I move them.'

Nell noticed that he didn't even have his anorak on. She was about to point this out, but instead she said, 'Can I tell Mum and Dad where you are, now?'

'I think you'd better,' said Will.

★

The next day Will was ill. He had a terrible cold, a big bruise on his forehead and he'd sprained both his ankles. The birthday party was put off for a week.

Nell went to give her brother his present. It was a book that he'd always wanted, about spaceships. Will was sitting up in bed. His nose was red and he had a big bump on his forehead. 'Wow, thanks,' he said when he'd opened his present. And then, dropping his voice, he whispered, 'Nell, could you climb up to the tree-house for me, the almost-tree-house?'

'Me? Why?' Nell was astonished.

'I left my anorak there and Gran's present's in the pocket.'

'You really want me to climb up to your almost-tree-house?' Nell had to make sure.

14

'*Yes!*' Will said, rather loudly this time. 'I can't get there 'cos I'm ill. But you're well, aren't you?'

'I'm always well,' said Nell.

A few minutes later she was climbing up to the tree-house platform. When she got there she stood still for a moment, gazing down at the house and the fields and, far away, the dark roofs of the village. It was a beautiful day, the wind had dropped and the sunshine warmed her face.

Nell smiled to herself. 'I got here,' she said. 'I got to the almost-tree-house.'

2. Will's new bicycle

One of Will's birthday presents was a new bicycle. He wasn't allowed outside on his birthday, so Mr Shepherd wheeled it into the yard beneath Will's window and shouted, 'Look, Will! A present to make up for the tree-house.'

Will's head ached and his throat was so sore it seemed as though he had swallowed broken glass. But the sight of the shiny red bike cheered him up. He waved at his dad and stuck his thumbs in the air. 'Thanks, Dad!' he croaked.

The next minute Nell was there, smiling

up at him and patting the bike's smart red saddle.

Mr Shepherd asked her to take it back into the garage but, as soon as she took the handle-bars, Will began  thumping on the window-pane. 'It's not yours,' he wheezed. 'Leave it alone.'

'I'm not going to ride it!' she shouted as she wheeled the bike away. She wished her brother wouldn't get so angry about things. 'One day he'll explode,' she muttered.

It was Saturday, and Nell was expecting her friend, Fiona, to come over in the afternoon. She always brought her wellies when she came to see Nell. 'That farm's such a mucky place,' her mother complained. Mrs Strange

was rather nervous about Fiona's visits to the Shepherds' farm. There were so many dangers: angry bulls, vicious cockerels, slippery paths, muddy dogs and duck ponds.

'Fiona mustn't do anything dangerous,' Mrs Strange told Mrs Shepherd.

'Of course not,' said Mrs Shepherd. 'I'm sure Fiona will be sensible.'

'Sometimes Nell leads her on, you know,' said Mrs Strange.

This wasn't true, but Nell and Mrs Shepherd didn't say anything. They were too polite to point out that it was the other way round.

When Mrs Strange had

gone, Nell and Fiona put on their wellies and went outside.

'What's that?' said Fiona when she saw the almost-tree-house.

Nell told her it was Will's tree-house. 'But it's not finished, yet,' she said.

'I'm going to climb that rope ladder,' said Fiona.

'Better not,' Nell advised. 'You might fall.'

'Nah,' said Fiona. She ran to the ladder and began to climb. One, two, three. She was three rungs up. The ropes swung about like snakes.

'Slower,' warned Nell. 'The rope ladder's very slippery.'

'Nah!' said Fiona. She lifted her foot for

the next step, but the heel of her wellie caught in the rope. For a moment Fiona wobbled and screamed, and then, THUMP, she was on the ground. Her jeans were all muddy and her knees were cut and bruised.

Nell took her indoors to get patched up, and that's where they stayed for the rest of the day. 'I think you'll be safer playing inside,' said Mrs Shepherd.

Mr Shepherd took Fiona home after tea. Before he got back there was a phone call for Mrs Shepherd. It was Fiona's mum.

'I don't want Fiona to come to the farm for a while,' Mrs Strange told Nell's mum. 'It's too risky. She's always having accidents.

Her knees are in a terrible state.'

'Nell's never had an accident,' said Mrs Shepherd.

'Nell can come to our house if she wants,' said Mrs Strange. 'I know she's Fiona's best friend.'

Nell didn't want to go to Fiona's house. Fiona had three little brothers who made a racket and followed them everywhere.

'I suppose I'll just have to stay at home with Will,' she said. Her dreams of a tea party in the tree-house were beginning to fade.

When he was better, the first thing Will wanted to do was to ride his new bike.

'Go carefully,' warned Mr Shepherd. 'It's much bigger than your old bike.'

'I'm always careful,' said Will.

His mum and dad and sister rolled their eyes.

'I'll just ride it down the lane to start with,' he said.

Nell went with him. She rode her pale blue bicycle with butterflies painted on the saddle, and she put on her safety helmet, just in case.

'You don't need that,' said Will. 'We're not going on the main road.'

'All the same,' said Nell. 'Accidents can happen.'

Jessie the sheepdog ran after the children, barking for joy. There was nothing she liked better than chasing bicycles. She was very unpopular with the postman.

After riding up and down the lane four times, Will wanted to try something different. 'I think I'll take the bike up the sheep-track to the top of the hill, and then whizz down,' he said. 'After all, it is a mountain bike.'

Nell thought the hill was rather steep, even for a mountain bike. She followed Will up to the fields and then watched him wheel his bike to the top of the hill. Jessie sat beside Nell with her ears pricked forward and her tail thumping, just as if she were expecting some excitement.

Nell hooked her finger in Jessie's collar. 'You can't chase Will this time,' she said. 'You'll cause an accident.'

Jessie looked up at Nell and whined.

'You can't race him either,' said Nell.

23

Will was slowing down now. The hill became very steep for the last few metres, too steep, Nell thought, for a bicycle. She wished Will would stop where he was and ride down. But on he went, pushing and puffing.

When Will was almost at the top of the hill, Nell saw the bullocks. They were coming round the side of the hill, six of them. They weren't as big as Mr Shepherd's prize bull, but they were lively and rough. Time and again, Mr Shepherd had told his children not to go into the bullocks' field. 'They're heavy animals,' he said, 'and very inquisitive. They don't mean to hurt, but when they're running they could knock you over in a second.'

'Look out, Will!' Nell called. 'Don't ride down, the bullocks are coming.'

Will took no notice. Perhaps he couldn't hear her. He turned his bike and swung his leg over the saddle.

24

'No, Will!' screeched Nell.

'Wheeeee!' cried Will as he came sailing down the track.

Jessie leaped up and down barking furiously. All at once she broke away from Nell and ran towards Will.

'Get out of the way!' Will yelled at the dog.

'Jess, come back!' cried Nell.

Will tried to slow down. Jessie was running up the track right in front of him. 'Jess!' he shrieked. He braked suddenly. The bike stopped, but Will didn't.

He flew over the handlebars and landed on his head.

Nell did some very quick thinking. I've got my helmet on, so I won't get hurt as badly as Will. She ran up to him, keeping an eye on the bullocks. They were very interested in Will's accident. In fact, they were pounding closer and closer.

'You've got to get up, Will!' Nell shouted. 'The bullocks are coming.'

Jessie ran at the bullocks, yelping and growling, but they took no notice. She was a sheep-dog, not a bull-dog. Her barking only made the bullocks more excited.

Nell reached her brother and pulled him to his feet. 'Now run,' she said. 'As fast as you can.'

'My bike,' moaned Will. 'I can't leave my bike.'

'I'll bring the bike,' said Nell. 'I've got a helmet on. You just run.'

Will limped as fast as he could towards the gate, while Nell pulled the bike upright and began to wheel it down after Will. Will's new bike was much heavier than hers, the handle-bars were high and awkward to hold and she found she couldn't run. She kept tripping up. The bullocks were snorting now, in a very unfriendly way. She could almost feel their breaths on her neck. She'd never make it to the gate if she didn't run faster.

Will had reached the gate and, as he swung himself on to the bars, he saw Nell and the bike. The bullocks were just a few metres behind her.

27

'Leave the bike, Nell!' he shouted. 'Or you'll be trampled!'

Nell didn't need telling a second time. She dropped the bike and ran. Behind her she heard a horrible scrunching noise as the bullocks ran over the bike. It seemed to hold them up a bit; just long enough for Nell, racing like the wind, to reach safety.

Will and Nell tumbled over the gate and dropped into the mud, just in time. The bullocks snorted at them, banging their heads on the bars and stamping in the muddy pools behind the gate.

Jessie didn't bother with the gate, she came flying over the wall, yelping in panic.

'It's your fault!' cried Will. 'You silly sheepdog. Look at my bike.'

The bullocks were playing with Will's brand new bike. It was a sorry sight. The spokes were broken, the saddle had come off and the handlebars were bent. It hardly

28

looked like a bike at all.

When Will and Nell staggered into the kitchen, Will was trying hard not to cry. His hair was full of mud and he had another bruise on his head.

'Whatever's happened?' cried Mrs Shepherd.

Out came the sad tale of the bullocks and the bike.

'My head aches,' moaned Will.

'What about you, Nell?' asked Mrs Shepherd. 'Were you hurt?'

'Not at all,' said Nell. 'I had my safety helmet on. I'm quite well.'

3. Two angry rams

Will felt much better in the morning. 'D'you think you could finish the tree-house today?' he asked his father.

'I haven't got time to build a tree-house,' said Mr Shepherd. 'There's too much to do.' He was trying to mend Will's bike. An impossible task.

'How about the day after that?' asked Will. 'I mean, it was supposed to be my birthday present.'

'I bought you a bike instead,' his dad reminded him.

'But my bike's all smashed up,' grumbled Will.

'And whose fault's that?'

Jessie gave a loud bark, almost as if she were owning up.

'It was Jessie's fault,' said Will, glaring at  the sheepdog. Jessie wagged her tail.

'No use blaming it on a dog,' said Mr Shepherd.

Will's new friend, Martin Doyle, had promised to bring his bike round on Saturday. They were going to ride all round the farm, maybe even do some tricks on the stone walls. Now Will hadn't got a bike to ride.

'You can borrow mine,' Nell offered.

'It's a girl's bike,' sniffed Will

Nell ignored this. 'What about your old bike?'

32

'It's not a mountain bike and both the tyres are flat,' Will said.

Nell didn't bother to suggest Will mend his tyres, even though she knew he'd done it before. She decided that her brother just wanted to be miserable. Perhaps his head still ached.

'You're lucky to have a friend,' Nell muttered. 'Fiona's mum won't let her come here any more.'

Will suddenly felt sorry for his sister. 'You can come round with Martin and me,' he said. 'As long as you just watch when we're doing dangerous stuff.'

Nell brightened up. She wondered what sort of dangerous stuff they might do. 'I'll just watch,' she promised.

On Saturday morning, Jessie's barking woke Nell up. Jessie only barked like that when strangers came into the yard. Nell got out of bed and ran to the window.

Standing just inside the gate was a boy with curly hair. He was holding tight to the handlebars of a shiny black bike. Jessie was running round him, snapping excitedly.

Nell opened the window. 'Stop that, Jessie!' she shouted. 'Leave him alone!'

Jessie whined and sat down.

The boy grinned up at Nell. 'Thanks,' he said. 'I'm Martin Doyle. I've come to see Will.'

Nell put on her slippers and ran down to open the door, but Will had already brought his friend into the kitchen. He'd had his breakfast and was keen to show Martin the farm.

'Please be careful, Will,' said Mrs Shepherd. 'Don't do anything silly. Martin isn't used to farms.'

'We'll be careful,' said Will.

What was all that talk about dangerous stuff? Nell ran upstairs to get dressed. After breakfast she decided to go and find the boys. She hoped Will hadn't changed his mind about her going round with them.

She found Will and Martin in the almost-tree-house. Mr Shepherd had managed to do a bit more work on it and now it had one whole wall of planks, as well as a floor. Martin was very impressed. 'You can see for miles,' he said. 'D'you want to come up, Nell?'

'There's no room,' Will said quickly. 'And she'd hurt herself climbing the rope ladder.'

'I've done it before,' Nell called up to him, 'when you wanted me to fetch your birthday present.'

Will took no notice. 'Let's go down and see the pigs,' he said.

For the rest of the morning, Nell followed Will and Martin round the farm. They looked at the tractors in the barn, climbed trees in the wood and took it in turns to ride Martin's bike down the lane. Will ignored Nell but at least he didn't tell her to go away. Now and again Martin looked back and gave her a smile, so it wasn't too bad. It would have been a lot better if she'd had her own friend to talk to, though.

After a while, Nell decided she didn't want to follow the boys any more. She went and sat on the swing, where she had a good view of the almost-tree-house. She imagined how it would look with a roof and a window, maybe even a chimneypot, just for show.

Mr Shepherd walked past, looking rather the worse for wear. 'I've had a bad time with those rams,' he told Nell. 'They're always so angry when I take them away from their wives.' He laughed and Nell felt

37

better. Every winter Mr Shepherd had to separate the rams and the ewes. The ewes would have their lambs soon after Christmas and the rams were very jealous.

The Shepherds had two rams; Nell called them Ralph and Rupert. Will couldn't tell them apart, but Nell would always know Ralph, she'd fed him with a bottle when he was just a lamb. He was bigger and stronger than Rupert and his horns were longer.

Nell thought she would take Ralph and Rupert a treat to cheer them up. They were very fond of little apples. There was a store of apples in the barn, and Nell went to choose two of the smallest.

Will and Martin had completely vanished and Nell felt slightly anxious about Martin. She hoped Will wasn't leading him into danger.

The sun was going down and a fine mist was beginning to creep over the hills. Soon it would be dark. Nell hurried up to the field where Ralph and Rupert spent the winter. She could hear a gate banging and she had an uncomfortable feeling that something was not quite right.

Nell could see the field now. Ralph and Rupert were standing together by the wall. The two boys were sitting on top of the gate and Will was banging the bars with his feet.

'Don't tease them!' Nell shouted. 'They're very angry today!'

As usual, Will paid no attention to her. In fact, quite distinctly, she heard him say, 'Come on!' and, to Nell's horror, Will

39

jumped into the field. Martin slid down after him.

Ralph and Rupert looked at the two boys and Nell could almost see the rams making up their minds: you go for Will and I'll get Martin.

Will began to run round the side of the field. Ralph lowered his head and charged. Rupert was just about to run at Martin when Nell reached the gate. She threw the apples into the field and Rupert hesitated, just long enough for Martin to hurl himself over the gate to safety.

'Phew!' he gasped. 'Will said those rams were friendly.'

'Not today,' said Nell.

Ralph was pounding after Will and

40

when Will tried to climb the wall, Ralph's horns caught up with his bottom. What happened next was quite spectacular. Will flew. With a bloodcurdling yell he soared into the air, his arms spread out like long skinny wings.

'Wow!' breathed Martin. 'That must have hurt.'

Will dropped on to the grass with a

moan. Luckily he was on the right side of the wall.

Nell and Martin helped Will back to the house. Will couldn't speak, he just kept moaning. When he got home he stumbled upstairs and lay on his bed, face down. Mrs Shepherd rang the doctor.

Martin's mother came to fetch him after tea and Mrs Shepherd explained what had happened. 'I'm afraid Will's always in the wars,' she said.

'What about Nell?' asked Mrs Doyle. 'Are you always in the wars, too?'

'No,' said Nell. 'I'm always well.'

'Ill Will and Well Nell,' laughed Martin.

Nell thought that Mrs Doyle would be cross about the rams. After all, Martin had been in danger, but she only said, 'Boys will be boys.'

'You saved me, Nell,' said Martin as he left. 'See you!'

When the Doyles had gone, Nell went to look at the almost-tree-house. Will would never know if she climbed into it now. He would be lying down for quite a while. Before she could change her mind, she scrambled up the ladder and sat on the platform. A big white moon was rolling up behind the hills and all the trees looked soft and silvery.

'What have you been up to?' asked Mrs Shepherd when Nell came in.

'Just thinking,' Nell said.

4. Chickenpox

Will was a striker in the school football team. He was just about the best player, as he scored all the goals. There was to be a very important match in two weeks' time but, with two big bruises on his bottom, Will found it hard to run. Without him the school might lose the match.

Each day Will found he could walk a little faster. After a week he could run. But could he run fast enough? And could he score a goal? Nell helped out. After

44

school she would play football with Will in the field behind the house. The one without the rams.

After another week, Mr Simms, the P.E. teacher, said Will was well enough to play in the match.

'Just in time,' Will told Nell. It was Thursday and the match was on Saturday.

That night Will said he had a bit of a headache.

'Nerves,' said Mr Shepherd. 'You'll be fine tomorrow.'

Will wasn't fine. In the middle of the night he was sick. Next morning when he came down to breakfast he had two spots on his forehead. Even as Nell watched, more began to appear.

45

'One of the boys in our class has got chickenpox,' said Nell. 'It looked just like that.'

'Oh dear!' Mrs Shepherd stared at Will. 'I think you've got it, Will.'

Will did have chicken-pox. He had to miss the football match and the school team lost. To cheer him up, Mr Shepherd promised to finish the tree-house. He worked on it all weekend.

Nell watched her dad nailing planks to the wooden platform. She stood beside the tree holding Mr Shepherd's toolbox and carrying the things he needed up the rope ladder.

The tree-house grew and grew. Soon there were four walls and a big space for a window. Next came the roof. This seemed to be the hardest part. Mr Shepherd's hammering rang out across the hills. It was a wonderful roof with beams and roofing-felt. Mrs Shepherd provided a small table, two chairs and a piece of carpet. The tree-house would be warm and dry inside.

In a few days Will felt better, but he wasn't allowed to go to school. Not that this worried him. He spent all his time in the tree-house. He pulled things up in a bucket attached to a pulley: soldiers, Lego, books, pencils, cars, marbles, and even a giant model of Darth Vader. Tiger, the cat, climbed up by himself. He'd decided to live there for a while.

'Have you got cups and saucers?' Nell asked.

'Why would I want them?' said Will. 'I can drink out of a bottle.'

Obviously he didn't plan to have a tea party.

Still, Nell had something to look forward to. Soon there was to be a school trip to Blainey castle. Her teacher, Mrs Tinker, had told them all about it. Nell loved castles. She loved the narrow, curving stairs, the huge stone towers and the deep, dark dungeons. She could almost see the archers on the battlements with their bows and arrows. She could imagine knights on white chargers thundering across the drawbridge, and medieval ladies in long, floaty dresses. Did

48

they use cups and saucers? Nell wondered. Or plates with flowers on them?

Mrs Tinker didn't want Will to come back to school until he was quite free of chickenpox. She was expecting a baby and she didn't want to catch anything nasty before the baby arrived. So, although Will didn't feel ill, he couldn't go to school. Two days before the school trip, the doctor said Will wasn't infectious any more.

'Just in time!' Will cried. 'I can go to Blainey castle, after all.'

Nell thought it was rather unfair that Will had been let off school for so long, and then got to go on the school trip. She wondered if

49

Will would fall in the moat, or tumble down one of the curving staircases. I'd better keep an eye on him, she thought, he's missed too much school already.

Next morning Nell woke up with a headache. It was just a little headache, not bad enough to make her miss the school trip. She got dressed and started to brush her hair. When she looked in her mirror she noticed a blob on her chin, there were two more on her forehead and another one on the bridge of her nose. Could they be spots?

'No,' whispered Nell. She had an idea. If she pulled her hair over her face no one would see the spots. She nearly fell down the stairs on her way to breakfast. She could hardly see a thing because she'd brushed her hair over her face instead of behind her ears.

'Nell, whatever have you done with your hair?' asked Mr Shepherd.

'It's the latest style,' said Nell. She tried to get a spoonful of Cornflakes through to her mouth, but missed and spilled them all over the table – and her hair.

'You can't see what you're doing.' Mrs Shepherd pulled Nell's hair away from her face. 'Oh, my goodness, you've got chickenpox!' she said.

'No,' wailed Nell.

'I'm afraid you have,' said her mum. 'You can't

possibly go to school today.'

'But I feel well!' cried Nell.

'You might get worse,' Mrs Shepherd told her. 'It's no good, Nell. If you go to school, Mrs Tinker will just send you home.'

Nell burst into tears. 'I want to go to Blainey castle,' she sobbed. 'I've been thinking about it for days and days.'

'I'm sorry, Nell,' said her mum.

'It's not fair,' cried Nell. 'It's all Will's fault. He gave me the chickenpox.'

She noticed that Will was staring at her in a very odd way. He looked really upset

52

about something. 'You can go in my tree-house,' he said. 'In fact, you can go there anytime you want, any, any time. I promise.'

'I don't want to go in the tree-house,' moaned Nell. 'I want to go to Blainey castle.'

It was no good. Nell's parents wouldn't let her go on the school trip. When Will left with his anorak and sandwiches, she muttered, 'I hope it rains,' and then changed her mind and called out, 'Have a good time!'

'I mean it about the tree-house!' Will called back.

Nell sat in the kitchen feeling very sorry for herself. 'I don't feel ill,' she told her mum. 'I'm never ill. I'm always well.'

The telephone rang and Mrs Shepherd picked up the receiver. 'Oh, I'm so sorry,' she said. 'What a shame. No, I'm afraid

Will's gone back to school. Never mind. Another time.' She put down the receiver and then frowned, the way she did when an idea was coming.

'That was Mrs Doyle,' she told Nell. 'Martin's got chickenpox, too, and he can't go on the school trip. Mrs Doyle wanted him to come and spend the day with Will. I was wondering . . . would you like Martin to come here?'

'If he wants,' said Nell. 'But he won't. He's Will's friend.'

'We'll see,' said her mum, and she rang Mrs Doyle.

Martin was very keen to spend the day at the farm. He didn't mind at all that Nell was at home and not Will. In fact he had a brilliant idea.

'Let's pretend we're at Blainey castle, hundreds of years ago,' he said.

'And you can be a knight!' cried Nell,

instantly cheering up. 'And I'll be a lady in a long floaty dress.'

'And the tree-house will be your tower,' said Martin.

'And Jessie can be your horse,' said Nell.

Later that morning, Nell and Martin climbed up to the tree-house.

Nell wore one of her mum's long dresses and a shawl for a cloak. Martin wore Will's grey balaclava and a long red towel. He left his horse beside the tree, with a bone to keep her quiet. When Nell pointed out that horses didn't eat bones, Martin said, 'It's not a bone, it's a parsnip.' He had a wonderful imagination.

Mrs Shepherd put a pot of tea in Will's pulley-bucket, with two cups and saucers, two flowery plates and a bag of ham sandwiches. Very carefully Nell pulled it up through the window. She set out the plates and cups on the table and began to pour the tea. But when Martin's cup was half full, she suddenly stopped pouring.

'You don't mind drinking out of a cup, do you?' she asked, thinking of Will.

'Not at all,' said Martin.

'Or eating off flowery plates?'

'Not a bit,' said Martin.

Everything Nell ate seemed to taste delicious, even the custard tarts that Martin had brought.

It began to rain and the gentle drumming of raindrops on the tree-house roof made it seem, somehow, all the more cosy.

'I reckon this is better than Blainey castle,' said Martin, happily licking his fingers.

Nell had to agree. Tea in the tree-house was even more wonderful than she had imagined.

For Emily,

J.N.

To Mish,

with much love,

A.B.

Contents

1 Matthew and the Beast

Tansy was afraid of birds. She knew it was silly, but she couldn't help it. 'Perhaps,' she said, 'when I was a baby, a bird flew into my pram and pecked me, or stole a toy.'

'No,' said Mrs Gray, Tansy's mum, 'Nothing like that ever happened.'

Tansy huddled deeper into the mound of bags on the back seat of the car. 'How d'you know it didn't happen?' she said. 'I could have been in the garden while you were indoors. So you wouldn't have seen it.'

'True,' her mum admitted, 'but it's unlikely. You'd have screamed.'

'You can't hear anything when the

2

vacuum cleaner's going,' Tansy muttered.

'*That's* true,' said Mr Gray. 'But whatever it is that makes you afraid of birds, you'll just have to get over it, Tansy. Because where we're going there'll be hundreds.'

'I know,' said Tansy sullenly. 'You told me.' She didn't mind the small birds, it was the large, dark birds she feared. The crows and rooks and jackdaws, birds that flocked together in a black cloud, cawing and shrieking.

Tansy's mum and dad had decided to change their lives. They gave up their work in the city and found something different in a country town.

They sold their flat in Station Road (where trains rumbled past all day) and bought half a house in the country, miles away from anywhere.

No one had asked Tansy what she wanted, but she told them anyway. 'I want to stay in Station Road,' she said, 'because I know everyone. I don't want to go somewhere strange and lonely.'

'You'll love it,' Dad said. 'You wait.'

And now, here they were, outside the new house, which looked very old, not new at all. It was a tall, grey-stone building with small windows and a very high chimney. On one side of the house strands of ivy hung over an upstairs window.

Tansy wondered which half of the

house was theirs. There were two front doors, two paths and two gardens separated by a thick hedge.

A boy came out of the house without the ivy.

Good, thought Tansy, I get the ivy.

'Oh, look, there's a boy next-door,' said Mrs Gray. 'He's about your age, Tansy. That's lucky.'

What's lucky? thought Tansy, boys are as bad as birds.

The boy had fair hair that flopped over his face, and he wore glasses. He clanged through the gate, came right up to the car and stared in at Tansy.

'Hullo!' He shouted as if she were miles away. 'I'm Matthew.'

'Oh,' mouthed Tansy.

Her dad climbed out of the car and shook Matthew's hand. Her mum did the same. Tansy stayed where she was.

'Come on, Tansy.' Mr Gray tapped on the window. 'Come and meet Matthew.' He opened the car door and Tansy reluctantly stepped out. Her dad said, 'This is Tansy. You'll be going to school together I expect.'

'Hi, Tansy!' said Matthew. 'I'm in Year Four. The bus stops right here. Are you coming to school tomorrow?'

'I . . .' Tansy began. She couldn't go on.

She heard her dad saying that she would be going to school by car on the first day, but after that she'd catch the bus with Matthew. And then Mr Gray saw Tansy's face.

'What's the matter, Tansy?' he said.

Tansy couldn't answer. She was staring at the roof. A shadow was settling over it; a chattering, cawing, murmuring cloud of birds.

'Birds,' whispered Tansy.

'Jackdaws,' said Matthew cheerfully. 'They live in the roof. We tried to get them out, but it's too late now; they've built their nests and laid their eggs. It wouldn't be fair.'

'It *isn't* fair,' said Tansy. 'It's not fair on me. I don't want to be here. I never did.' And she got back into the car and slammed the door.

The jackdaws were swooping in and out of the ivy, right above the window of the room that Tansy had decided would be hers.

Her mum and dad seemed very interested in Matthew. They ignored Tansy and began to pull things out

8

of the boot. Matthew helped. They walked up to the new front door, Mum, Dad and Matthew, carrying bags and cases, and they all went into the new-old house.

Tansy stayed where she was, but after a moment she began to feel silly. So she got out of the car and walked through the gate. She took three steps up the path, and then it happened. Something dark floated through the air and landed on a plum tree, right beside her.

Tansy glanced quickly at the tree. A bird sat there, swaying on a branch. It had a feathery grey hood and bright, pearl-grey eyes. It turned its head and stared at Tansy, and Tansy ran.

'Where are you?' Tansy cried, leaping through the front door.

'Here!' came Mum's voice.

Tansy tore down a dark passage towards the voice, and tumbled into a sunny kitchen.

Mum and Dad were filling the cupboards and Matthew was handing tins and packets of food to them. Tansy was annoyed to see the strange boy making himself at home in her new kitchen, but she kept quiet about it. She didn't mention the bird, either. She didn't want Matthew to laugh at her.

10

'I'm going to look at the rest of my new house,' she said. But at that moment the removal van turned up, and four large men in green overalls began to carry furniture into the house.

The passages and stairs in the house were very narrow, and it was quite a struggle to get everything in.

'Look out, Tansy! You'll get squashed,' yelled Dad as Tansy ducked behind a wardrobe.

'Tansy, you're in the way,' Mum shouted, as Tansy squeezed herself against the wall.

'You can come round to my house, if you like, while all this is going on,' said Matthew.

Tansy didn't want to go with Matthew, but she didn't want to get trampled to bits or squashed like a pancake, either, so she followed Matthew round to his side of the house. The bird, she noticed, had gone.

'This is Tansy,' said Matthew to his mum, who had just baked a cake.

Mrs Hood seemed to know who Tansy was. 'I was going to take this cake in to your mum,' she said. 'Moving house is a terrible business, isn't it?' She offered Tansy a piece of cake.

Tansy was starving. She took it, mumbling, 'Thanks.'

She'd barely taken two mouthfuls when Matthew said, 'Come and see my pets.'

Mrs Hood smiled. 'Go on Tansy. Don't worry about crumbs.'

Tansy followed Matthew into the back garden. He had two rabbits and four guinea pigs. They all lived together in a house a bit like a kennel. There was a long wire cage attached to it, almost as tall as Tansy. The rabbits were black and the guinea pigs were multicoloured. All the animals were out on the floor of the cage, nibbling: grass, carrots, a cabbage stalk, nuts and

seeds. It seemed to be their teatime, too.

At the end of the Hoods' back garden, a wall rose behind a bed of flowers. It ran all the way past the hedge and on into the garden next-door: Tansy's garden. Beyond the wall a green field sloped gently up to a row of trees. There wasn't another house in sight.

'It really is different,' murmured Tansy. She couldn't remember when she'd last seen a place without houses.

As she stared over the long stone wall, a huge ginger cat bounced on to it; as if from nowhere.

'Buzz off!' yelled Matthew. 'Go on. Go away!'

The big cat just glared at him.

'Don't shout at it,' said Tansy. 'It's only a cat.'

'It's the Beast,' said Matthew. 'Shove off!' he shouted at the cat again. 'We call him the Beast because he's fierce and cruel and greedy.'

'Where does he come from?'

'He used to live with an old lady in your house,' said Matthew. 'But when the old lady died, the Beast ran away. He's gone kind of wild. No one can catch him. He lives on mice and rats and things. I hate him. He even catches birds and eats them.'

Privately, Tansy thought this was no bad thing, but she realised Matthew was fond of birds.

Eventually the Beast ran off, but not before hissing at Matthew in a very loud and scary voice.

Time passed quickly in Matthew's garden. There were so many things to

16

 see: a pond full of goldfish, stick insects in a shed, newts with golden bellies and four white hens in a long pen. One of the hens had laid an egg in the nesting box, and Matthew pressed it, still warm and slightly damp, into Tansy's hand.

'Have it for breakfast,' he said.

And then Tansy's mum was calling her from the kitchen window, and Tansy said, 'Thanks for the egg. I'd better go now.'

'You can come round any time,' said Matthew. 'Come tomorrow.'

Tansy said,
'I'll think about
it.'

When she
got back to
her side of
the house,
the removal
men had

gone, and Mum and Dad were in the
living room, arranging the furniture. It
looked strange in the new room.

'You seem to be getting on well with
Matthew,' said Mrs Gray.

'Matthew's all right,' said Tansy, 'but
he hates this big ginger cat because it's
wild. He calls it the Beast. It used to

live here. This is its home. So I'm going to make it tame again.'

2 Beak and Whisker

Tansy's mum took her upstairs to look at the bedrooms. 'We thought you'd like this room,' said Mum, opening a door.

Tansy looked in. She saw ivy, prettily framing a window. Suddenly a bird, its wide wings dark against the sky,

20

swooped up into the roof above the ivy. And Tansy heard the high-pitched shrieking of hungry baby birds.

'No,' said Tansy, 'Not this room.'

'But the other room's smaller, and this one has such a pretty window,' said Mrs Gray.

'I don't like it,' said Tansy. 'All that horrible squeaking in the roof. I'll never sleep.'

'Birds sleep too,' said Mum, 'and

soon the baby birds will grow up and fly away.'

'Please, Mum! I want the other room.'

Mrs Gray gave a big sigh. 'All right.'

Tansy's new bedroom was small, but it had advantages. She could look down into Matthew's garden. She could watch the rabbits and guinea pigs, and even make out the quick flash of the goldfish in the pond. She would be very happy in this room, she decided.

Next day Mrs Gray took Tansy to school. It was a very small school, not what Tansy was used to at all. But the teachers were helpful, and most of the children were friendly, especially a girl called Isobel.

Isobel was taller than Tansy. She had long fair hair, very straight and silky. Tansy had always wanted straight

hair. Isobel took Tansy's hand and showed her round. It was a bit confusing coming to a new school in the middle of the summer term, but Isobel made it easier.

Tansy didn't see much of Matthew. He was in her class but he spent most of his time with a boy called Mark.

At the end of school, Tansy's mum came to fetch her.

'How did it go?' asked Mrs Gray.

'OK,' said Tansy. 'There's a nice girl called Isobel.'

'Good,' said Mum. 'Would you like to go on the bus tomorrow?'

'Yes,' said Tansy. 'Isobel goes on the bus.'

When Tansy got home, she arranged her new school books on the bedroom windowsill. She was just putting the last book in place, when something caught her eye. The big ginger cat had jumped on to the garden wall. It crouched down with its paws tucked in

24

and its tail flat on the stone.

Tansy ran downstairs. What would a cat like to eat? She took a small lump of cheese from the fridge.

'Where are you off to?' called Mrs Gray, as Tansy ran out of the kitchen.

'I'm going to feed the cat.'

She walked towards the wall. The ginger cat watched her. When she came close the cat began to growl.

'Stop complaining,' said Tansy. 'I've got some food for you.'

The big cat had an interesting face: a torn ear, a scratched nose, and one very long whisker sprouting from his eyebrow.

'Look out!' called a voice. 'The Beast will bite you!' It was Matthew, leaning out of his bedroom window.

'No, he won't,' said Tansy. 'He's just hungry.'

At that moment, the cat gave a hiss and a shriek. He stood and arched his back and spat at Tansy. Tansy dropped the cheese and ran back to the house.

'I don't think you're going to tame that cat,' said her mum. 'It's very fierce.'

The Beast had jumped off the wall and was biting into the cheese.

'I will,' said Tansy. 'You'll see.'

Next morning Tansy and Matthew got on the bus together. Isobel had saved Tansy a seat, and Matthew sat behind them.

'You shouldn't feed the Beast,' Matthew said, leaning over and breathing in Tansy's ear.

'He's not a beast. He's got a name.' Tansy leant away from Matthew. 'He's called Whisker.'

'Hunh!' Matthew sat back.

Tansy told Isobel about the cat. 'Poor cat,' said Isobel. 'It's sad he hasn't got a home of his own.'

'He will have – soon,' said Tansy.

Whisker didn't appear for several days, then, on Saturday when Tansy was helping her mum peg up the washing, there he was, looking rather the worse for wear. He sat on the wall, licking his paw and brushing

it over his torn ear.

'What can I give him, Mum?' asked
Tansy.

'There's some fish left over from
yesterday,' said Mrs Gray. 'I'm sure
he'd like that.'

He did.

This time Tansy managed to get right up to the wall. When Whisker began to grumble and growl, she dropped the fish beside him and jumped back. Whisker seized the fish and ran off.

'It's working!' Tansy gave a jump of excitement. Then she looked round to see if Matthew had been watching. But he was nowhere to be seen.

On Sunday, Tansy stood by her window and watched Matthew clean out his animals. She wished she could help, but she wasn't sure if he was friendly any more, because of Whisker.

Her dad called her downstairs.

'Tansy, there's a funny noise outside the window. Can you hear it?'

Tansy could. It was a loud squawking noise. She had a very good idea what it was. 'No, I can't hear anything,' she muttered.

'I can.' Mrs Gray looked up from her paper. 'It sounds like a baby bird. Tansy, go and have a look.'

Tansy opened the front door and peeped out. A dark thing fluttered in the grass below the living-room window. High above, a jackdaw looked out of the ivy and called to its child.

The fluttering thing screeched. Tansy froze.

'Tansy, quick!' Matthew looked over the hedge. 'Do something.'

'You do it,' she said.

'You're nearer,' cried Matthew. 'Look out! The Beast will get it.'

And there was the Beast, Tansy's Whisker, creeping over the lawn towards the fluttering thing.

'TANSY!' yelled Matthew, racing to his gate.

Tansy almost jumped out of her socks. Before  she knew what she was doing, she found herself hopping over the grass. Whisker

was about to pounce, but Tansy pounced first. She picked up the bony, shrieking creature and clasped it to her chest, while a growling Whisker glared up at her.

'Well done!' Matthew came running up to Tansy and reached for the bird.

'Ugh!' Tansy placed the struggling, half-feathered bundle into Matthew's hands.

A disgusted Whisker marched away from them.

'What are you going to do with it?'

Tansy asked Matthew.

'Well, the mother can't feed it down here,' he said. 'And if we put it back in the nest, it'll probably fall out again.'

'So you'll have to feed it.'

'Yes. I've done it before. Not with a baby jackdaw, though.' Matthew looked doubtful, which was unusual for him.

'Good luck,' said Tansy.

She went back indoors and told her parents.

'He's very good with animals, isn't he?' said Tansy's mum.

'Not cats,' said Tansy.

She tried to forget the baby bird, but she couldn't stop wondering how

Matthew was going to feed it. Perhaps it had died? That afternoon, curiosity got the better of Tansy. 'I'm going next-door to see Matthew,' she told her mum.

She went round and knocked on the Hoods' front door. Mrs Hood seemed to know why she had come. 'D'you want to see the bird?' she asked.

'I just wondered . . .'

'Come in,' Mrs Hood smiled. 'Matthew's just feeding it.'

As she went down the passage Tansy could hear a high-pitched squawking.

Matthew was in the kitchen, kneeling beside a small wicker shopping basket. He had what looked like a piece of

34

worm in his fingers. As Tansy peered
into the basket, Matthew dropped
whatever it was into a huge yellow
beak. There was silence as the bird
swallowed.

'I think it's had enough,' said Matthew.

'What did you give it?'

'Cut-up worm.'

'Uuurgh!' Tansy felt sick.

'Mum's going to get some tins of cat food,' Matthew told her. 'Jackdaws need meat you see, but only in tiny bits.'

'But to . . . to do what you did to a worm. That's disgusting.'

'It had to be done,' said Matthew. 'And I'll probably have to do it again.'

Tansy looked closer into the basket. The baby jackdaw had bright blue eyes. Its bony-

looking wings

were only

partly feathered,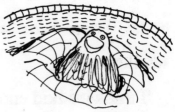

and the two halves of its beak were outlined in a fierce yellow. Even closed, the beak looked large. In fact the whole bundle looked big for a baby.

'I thought baby birds were tiny,' she murmured.

'Jackdaws are big birds,' said Matthew.

'How long are you going to feed it?'

'Until it can fly. That could take weeks. Its wings haven't grown yet. I'm going to call it Beak.'

'Beak?' exclaimed Tansy. 'You can't call it Beak. It should have a real name like Joe, or Bill or Jack.'

'Beak,' said Matthew firmly. 'It's my jackdaw.'

'I rescued it.'

Matthew went quiet. Tansy could see he wasn't going to change his mind.

'Tell you what,' Tansy said. 'If you call the Beast Whisker, I'll call the bird Beak.'

'Done!' said Matthew.

They shook hands. The baby jackdaw watched with bright blue eyes. And then it closed its silvery lids and fell asleep. Safe and full.

3 The night of the full moon

Tansy told Isobel about the bird. It was Monday morning and they were sitting on the bus. The cut-up worm wasn't mentioned. Tansy didn't think that would have been fair to Matthew.

'So what does it eat?' asked Isobel.

'Matthew's mum got some cat food,'

said Tansy.

Behind them, Matthew listened with a big grin on his face.

'Why don't you get some cat food for Whisker?' said Isobel.

Of course. Why hadn't Tansy thought of it? 'It's a great idea,' she said.

Matthew looked a bit worried when he got off the bus that afternoon.

Mrs Gray and Mrs Hood were chatting by the fence, as usual.

'I hope Mum remembered to feed Beak,' said Matthew. 'It's really important. He could die if he doesn't get enough food.'

Tansy hoped Mrs Hood didn't have to go and find worms. 'Does he wake up in the night?' she asked. Her mum had warned her that babies did this.

'Nope. He slept right through,' said Matthew proudly.

Tansy's mum suddenly held up a tin. 'I've got some cat food for Whisker,' she said.

'Mum, you're brilliant,' cried Tansy. 'I was going to ask.'

'D'you want to come and see Beak?' Matthew asked Tansy.

'Maybe. When I've fed Whisker.'

But Whisker didn't appear. Tansy spooned some cat food on to a saucer and put it on the wall. Then she waited. Waited and waited.

He's offended, thought Tansy. He wanted the baby bird and I wouldn't let him have it.

She decided not to go and see Beak. She wouldn't visit the jackdaw until she saw Whisker again.

Next morning the cat food had gone.

'He did come back, then,' said Tansy's mum. 'You just didn't see him.'

'It could have been another cat,' Dad pointed out. 'Or even a bird.'

'A jackdaw!' shrieked Tansy. 'A jackdaw stole Whisker's food!'

Mrs Gray told Tansy to calm down. They couldn't be certain.

Every day for a week, Tansy put a saucer of food on the garden wall. But Whisker never appeared. Tansy took the saucer in at night, in case a jackdaw got it.

On Saturday morning, Matthew looked over the hedge and asked Tansy why she hadn't been to see Beak.

'Because Whisker has disappeared,' said Tansy. 'I put some food out for him, but a jackdaw ate it.'

'Jackdaws don't eat cat food,' said Matthew. 'Not when they can get things that move: beetles and flies and moths and things.'

'Then why are you giving cat food to Beak?' asked Tansy.

'Because he can't catch his own food yet. And you wouldn't like me to spend my time cutting up worms, would you?'

'No,' Tansy agreed.

'Leave some food on the wall tonight,' said Matthew, 'and then keep watch. There's going to be a full moon.'

'There might not be.'

'Trust me,' said Matthew. 'I know these things. Got to go now. Come round tomorrow.'

'I'll think about it,' said Tansy.

There *was* a full moon that night. An orange moon. It appeared very early above the hill. And then it rose into the sky getting paler as the sky darkened. Tansy put the saucer of food on the wall before she went to bed. And then she watched from her bedroom window.

But she couldn't keep her eyes open. Her head sank back on to the pillow, and she fell asleep. When she woke up the moon was staring into her face.

Tansy knelt beside the window and looked out.

She'd caught him. There on the wall was the ginger cat, enjoying his meal.

Every night after that, Tansy put a saucer of food on the wall. Sometimes she saw Whisker, and sometimes she fell asleep before he arrived. But it gave her a good feeling to know that the wild cat's visits were becoming a habit.

He rarely appeared in daylight. Mrs Gray said he probably slept all day and worked at night. Cats were like that. They slept for eighteen hours out of twenty-four. Much longer than a human being.

Tansy began to visit Matthew. She told herself it was the rabbits she wanted to see, and the fat little guinea pigs. But she couldn't help taking a peep at the jackdaw. It was amazing how fast he had grown. Soon his wings were covered in sleek black feathers; his beak lost its fierce yellow and became slimmer and darker. He began to tumble out of his basket and flutter about, but still he couldn't fly.

Mrs Hood made Matthew find a bigger box and move Beak into the back porch. A young jackdaw was too messy for a kitchen. Matthew fixed a bamboo cane across the box and Beak would perch there, watching things. Whenever he saw Matthew, he would flap his

wings excitedly and
call for food.

Sometimes Matthew
took Beak for a walk
in the garden. Beak
would sit on his arm,
turning his head to
stare at the ground, looking for insects.

And then Beak began to walk. He
would stride across the garden, peering
under stones, pecking at anything that
moved. He was especially fond of
woodlice. One hot Saturday, Matthew
put a shallow dish of water on the lawn
and Beak leapt into it. His two
wings flew round like the sails of
a windmill while water flew in all

directions. He looked so funny, Tansy couldn't stop laughing.

Of course it was rather risky, letting a non-flying jackdaw strut round a garden, but Matthew was always watching. And then, one day, he didn't.

Isobel had come to visit Tansy. They ate their tea outside, sitting on the stone steps that led down to the lawn. Tansy was just biting into a ham sandwich when Whisker appeared on the wall.

'It's your cat,' cried Isobel. 'Shall we feed it?'

'Don't scare him,' Tansy warned.

'We'll just walk up to him, really slowly, and put a sandwich on the wall.'

The two girls crept forward. Whisker watched them, but he didn't move. The girls reached the wall and Tansy slowly lifted her sandwich and placed it in front of Whisker. He didn't growl. He

51

stared at Tansy suspiciously, then he bent his head to lick the sandwich. Tansy had been longing to touch him. Now was her chance. Her hand came up and she patted his back.

With a hiss and a spit, Whisker leapt away. He ran to the end of the wall and jumped down into Matthew's garden.

Horror of horrors! Tansy saw Beak strolling down the path. Whisker saw him too. He crouched, ready to spring.

Where was Matthew?

'Matthew! Matthew!' shrieked the girls.

The television was on in Matthew's house. He couldn't hear them. He was watching a programme about

robots, and the background music
was very loud.

Whisker was in killing mode: belly on the ground, one paw moving very, very slowly, and then the other.

Tansy screamed, 'Go away!' She could hardly believe what she had said, but she had to do it. 'Go away!'

Isobel clapped her hands and shouted, 'Shoo! Shoo!'

Whisker took no notice. He was intent on his prey. The prey knew nothing about it. The prey couldn't fly. The prey didn't stand a chance.

Unless . . .

Suddenly, Beak looked up. He turned his head to one side and stared at Whisker, curious and then interested. The girls couldn't believe their eyes. Beak took a step towards Whisker.

Whisker couldn't believe it either. Small creatures usually ran away from him. He wasn't used to being stared at, and then approached. Whisker didn't know what to do.

At that moment Matthew appeared, 'Did somebody . . .?'

The girls pointed, frantic and silent. But Matthew had already seen Beak and Whisker. With a mighty yell, he rushed down the path.

Whisker leapt on to the wall and

over it. Beak walked into a flower-bed and peeped out. Still curious.

'How did that happen?' Matthew lifted Beak out of the flowers.

'It wasn't our fault,' said Tansy. 'Someone left your door open and Beak just walked out.'

'It was Mum. She's always forgetting.' He ran indoors.

Tansy wished and wished she hadn't shouted at Whisker. 'He won't trust me now,' she grumbled.

'What else could you do?' said Isobel. 'You were trying to save a bird's life.'

'Beak can take care of himself,' Tansy muttered. 'That's obvious.'

It was the last week of term. Everyone was talking about their summer holidays. But the Grays weren't having a holiday. 'We've moved house, that's enough excitement for one year,' said Mr Gray.

Tansy noticed that Matthew's rabbits and guinea pigs had gone. Their cage was empty. She saw Mr Hood and Matthew fixing a long pole across the cage. What was going on?

'Where are your rabbits?' Tansy called over the hedge.

Mr Hood was hammering.

'Come round and I'll tell you,' Matthew shouted. Beak looked up from his shoulder.

Tansy ran round to the Hoods' front door and Mrs Hood let her in. There were cases in the hall, neatly folded coats and a row of shoes.

'We're going to America on Saturday,' said Mrs Hood. 'A holiday of a lifetime. My sister lives there. But our cases don't seem to hold enough for five weeks.'

'Five weeks is a long time,' Tansy remarked.

'It is.' Mrs Hood looked very happy about it.

Mr Hood had finished his work on the cage. He looked very pleased with himself.

'What's happening?' asked Tansy.

'We're going to put Beak in here while we're on holiday,' said Matthew. 'He'll be safe, and he's got lots of room to flutter about, and even a place to sleep. He can perch on the pole Dad's fixed up.'

'Where are your rabbits?'

'Mark's looking after them.'

'Is he going to come and feed Beak?' asked Tansy.

'No, he can't do that. He lives too far away.'

'So who's . . .?' Tansy had a sinking feeling.

'You'll look after Beak, won't you?' said Matthew.

'Me?' cried Tansy. 'I can't. I can't look after a bird.

I'm not a bird person.'

'Yes, you are,' said Matthew. 'You just won't admit it.'

4 Tansy and Beak

'I'm a cat person, not a bird person,'
wailed Tansy. 'I won't look after Beak,
I won't.' She stood in the middle of the
kitchen, grunting at her mum. 'How
am I supposed to tame a cat, if I'm
looking after a bird?'

'Calm down, Tansy. If you won't do

it, then I suppose I shall have to.' Her mum sighed. 'I promised to feed the chickens anyway. But we'll get a reward for that – new-laid eggs.'

Tansy calmed down. She felt mean. Her mum looked tired. 'All right, I'll do it,' she mumbled. 'I'd better go and find out *how* to do it.'

She went round to see Matthew again. He was kneeling beside Beak's new home looking rather glum.

'I don't think I want to go on holiday,' he said miserably. 'Something awful might happen to Beak.'

Tansy found herself saying, 'No it won't. I'll look after him.'

'Really?' Matthew looked more cheerful.

'Yes, really,' said Tansy, 'but you'd better show me how.'

Matthew explained things in rather a rush, and at first it sounded as though Tansy would be busy all day. The list of bird-chores was very long. There was  the bowl of water that had to be filled, the cat food that had to be minced up, the crumbs and tiny bits of cheese that had to be  scattered on the floor of the cage, and the hay in the nest that had to be changed once a week. 'And you'll have to scrub the perch now and again,' said Matthew. 'It gets a bit yucky.'

Tansy could have done without that last chore. 'Right,' she said, gritting her teeth. At least she wasn't going to have to cut up worms.

'He still likes to be fed by hand,' Matthew added wistfully. 'He gets a bit lonely.'

'Hm.' Tansy wasn't going to commit herself any further.

'Thanks, anyway,' said Matthew. 'We're leaving very early tomorrow, so in case you forget something, I'll write it all down and put the list through your letterbox.'

'Don't worry about a thing. You just go and have a good holiday.' Tansy skipped home, trying not to think about the problems tomorrow might bring.

By the time Tansy woke next morning, the Hoods had left. She looked out of the window. There was the cage, and there was Beak on his perch. Waiting. For her.

Downstairs she found the list Matthew had dropped through the letterbox.

'Now or never,' Tansy said to herself. She ran up to her room, dressed quickly and went round to the Hoods' back porch. The tins of cat food were stacked inside the door. An old spoon lay on top of the little tin bowl beside them. Tansy pulled back the ring on a tin marked 'Lamb' and spooned the meat into the bowl.

When she had minced up the cat food, she carried it down to the cage.

Beak saw her coming and he danced along the perch, flapping his wings excitedly. Tansy took a deep breath and opened the door. As she put the food in, Beak did something unexpected. He jumped on to Tansy's wrist. She froze.

'Mum! Mum!' squeaked Tansy.

Mrs Gray had just come in to the garden to feed the hens. 'What is it?'

'He's . . . he's on my hand,' said Tansy. 'Oooooo!'

'He won't hurt,' said her mum.

Beak took no notice of Tansy's squeaks. He perched comfortably on her wrist and pecked at the meat in the bowl.

Tansy dropped the bowl. A surprise for Beak. He turned his head

questioningly, and then dropped down to eat the spilt food. He also tried to lift the bowl. Tansy withdrew her hand and bolted the door quickly.

Later on she scattered crumbs through the wire at the top of the cage. That wasn't so risky. Now and again, throughout the day, Tansy would hear Beak calling: a sad and rather demanding squawk. But she tried not to hear the birdcalls. Her job was to feed and clean. Nobody said anything about making friends.

There had been no sign of Whisker since Tansy shooed him away. But she still put cat food on the wall at night, and something was eating it. Cat, bird, squirrel or rat? Nobody really knew.

For the next few days Tansy followed Matthew's list very carefully. She got used to Beak hopping on to her hand, and, although she wouldn't admit it, Beak's excited greeting rather pleased her. She was beginning to feel a bit lonely. Isobel was on holiday too, and the village was far away.

On Friday evening, Mr Gray said, 'We're

going to the seaside tomorrow!'

'Really!' cried Tansy. 'For a holiday?'

'Just for the day,' said her dad. 'I think we all deserve a treat, don't you?'

Tansy remembered Beak. What should she do about feeding him?

'Put a day's supply of food in his cage,' Mum said. 'I'm sure he'll be all right. He's a big bird now.'

So, on Saturday morning, Tansy put a large bowl of cat food in the corner of Beak's cage. She scattered crumbs on the floor as well. Beak watched her inquisitively. Tansy noticed that his round blue eyes were changing colour. Gradually they were turning pearly grey.

'Goodbye,' said Tansy. 'We're off to the seaside.'

It was the best day she'd had for ages. The sun was hot and the beach was perfect. Tansy spent all her time running in and out of the sea, fishing for shrimps and building sandcastles. Now and then she

poured water over her
mum and dad, to keep
them cool.

It was still light when they got home,
but very late. Tansy went round to see
Beak. He wasn't on his perch. He
wasn't near his bowl of food which was
half full. Tansy began to panic. Where
was Beak?

She saw a dark form in a corner.
Tansy crawled into the cage and

touched it. She felt soft, warm feathers, but there was no movement. Gently, she lifted the bird off the ground. Beak's silky lids were half-closed, and his head lolled forward.

'Oh, Beak, what is it?' Tansy whispered. 'What's the matter?'

And then she noticed that the water bowl was empty. She had forgotten to water, and it was at the top of Matthew's list.

'I'm sorry, I'm sorry,' Tansy sobbed.

'Tansy, what are you doing?' Mrs Gray peered into the cage.

'Oh, Mum, I think Beak's dying.'

Tears rolled down Tansy's cheeks. 'I forgot the water, and it was so hot today.'

'Bring him inside,' said Mrs Gray.

Carefully cradling the bird, Tansy crawled out of the cage and followed her mother into their kitchen.

Mrs Gray wet a finger and held a drop of water close to the bird's black beak. He gave a faint cheep. She tried again and he opened his beak. Next she held out a spoonful of water, and this time Beak sipped for himself, putting his head back and letting the water trickle down his throat.

'Mum,' breathed Tansy. 'You've done it. You've saved him.'

'Let's try some food,' said Mum.

Beak pecked a few bits of foods from Mrs Gray's hand, and then he half-closed his eyes. Slowly, he moved along Tansy's arm. When he reached the crook of her elbow, he tucked his head into her sleeve, and Tansy could almost feel a tiny sigh escape from him, before he fell asleep. The top of his head was crowned with tiniest of black feathers.

Tansy hardly dared to move. She sat in the kitchen with Beak tucked into her

arm as if he belonged there, and only when she was sure that he was sleeping peacefully, not ill or dead, Tansy laid him gently into the nest of hay at the back of his cage. Perhaps it wasn't just water that he had needed. Perhaps, he had been lonely.

Next morning Beak woke Tansy with his usual chirpy calls for food. This time Tansy brought him right out of the cage. She walked round the garden while he perched on her arm. She sat on the stone steps and he ran on to the lawn, picking at ants, woodlice, beetles and flies. Tansy kept an eye on the wall. Just in case Whisker decided to appear.

'If only you could fly, you'd be safe,' Tansy told the bird.

She'd noticed that the other young jackdaws had begun to fly. They would flutter out of the ivy and follow their parents into the trees, chattering with excitement. They were very noisy birds.

Beak had no one to teach him how to fly. 'It'll have to be me,' said Tansy. 'Otherwise you'll never learn.'

She picked him up and when he'd settled on her wrist, she swung her arm, very gently. Beak took off, his wings flapping wildly. Then he plummeted to the ground.

Every day after that, Tansy took Beak for a flying lesson, and every day he managed to flutter a little further. And then, one bright afternoon, he flew

right down the garden and landed on the roof of the chicken shed.

'Well done,' said Tansy, with a tiny pang of sadness.

Beak flew on, into the trees where his brothers and sisters were calling.

At teatime Tansy was quite tearful. When Mum asked her why she was upset, Tansy said, 'Beak can fly.'

'That's wonderful,' said Mrs Gray. 'Matthew will be impressed.'

Beak was a flyer now. He wouldn't go back into the cage, but he still came to Tansy for food. She didn't know where he slept. Perhaps he sat in the trees with his head tucked under his wing, or nestling among the other jackdaws. But wherever he went, he always came back in the morning, shouting for breakfast.

Sometimes he would land on Tansy's shoulder, and sometimes on her head. And she found that she wasn't afraid of dark wings swooping any more.

One day Beak didn't come back.

'He will,' said Tansy's mum. 'You'll see.'

But two days passed and there was no sign of him. Only a week to go and Matthew would be home. How was Tansy going to explain?

'Beak can fly. He's free. He's happy,' said Mrs Gray. 'Matthew will be glad for him.'

'No, he won't,' said Tansy. 'He'd want to be the one who let Beak go. He'd want to say goodbye.'

She walked round the garden, calling Beak's name and making frantic jackdaw sounds. But the flocks of chattering birds that flew overhead took no notice.

Tansy was looking into the sky when she almost tripped over a furry mound by the wall. Whisker had returned. Tansy had been leaving his food out every night, but she'd givenup watching for him. Now, here he was, fast asleep, at her feet.

She bent down, very slowly, and touched the cat's head. Whisker opened his eyes. He didn't growl. He didn't run away.

'Wait there,' Tansy said softly. She ran indoors and spooned some cat food into a saucer.

'Has Beak come back?' asked her mum.

'No. It's Whisker.' Tansy carried the saucer down to the bottom of the garden. Whisker hadn't moved. But when the food arrived he sat up and ate it, very noisily. And when Tansy risked another quick pat on his head, he didn't seem to mind too much.

In three days, Whisker has taken his first nervous steps back into his old home. In four days, Tansy was stroking him. On the fifth day, he purred. At the end of the week he spent the night in a cosy box in the Grays' back porch.

Beak had left, but Whisker had returned to take his place. If a nasty

little suspicion crossed Tansy's mind, she banished it, instantly.

The day that Tansy had been dreading arrived. The Hoods came back from their holiday. They drove up on a drizzly morning, and Matthew immediately rushed out into the garden. Tansy watched from her window. She saw Matthew peer into the empty cage. And then he began to call her.

'Tansy! Tansy, where's Beak?' He looked up at the window, and it was too late for Tansy to hide.

Dragging her feet, not knowing how she could explain, Tansy went round to Matthew's house.

Mrs Hood let her in with a cheerful smile. 'Hullo, Tansy. We've got a present for you.'

'Thanks,' Tansy smiled back. 'I've got to see Matthew,' she said, 'about the bird.' She made her way though the house and out into the garden.

'Where's Beak?' Matthew demanded.

Tansy explained, as best she could, about the flying lessons. 'I'm sorry you weren't here to say goodbye to him,' she said.

Matthew looked suspicious. And then something unfortunate happened. Whisker appeared and rubbed his head against Tansy's leg.

'What's he doing here?' said Matthew.

'Whisker's tame again. Isn't it good.'

'No, it's not good,' said Matthew, his voice rising. 'He's eaten Beak, hasn't he?'

'No! No!'

'Yes, he has. And you know it!'

'I don't. He wouldn't.' But Tansy

couldn't be sure, that was
the trouble.

'He's a beast, that
cat, and he always
will be!'

'It's not true,'
said Tansy,
fighting back the tears.

'Don't lie. Don't you ever . . .'
Matthew's mouth suddenly dropped
open. He looked really peculiar.

Tansy was hardly aware of the soft
touch in her hair, as she sobbed, 'I
couldn't keep Beak in a cage, could I?
Not when he could fly?'

Matthew just stared at her head.

Tansy put up her hand and felt two

twig-like legs. Beak stepped on to her wrist. Gently, she brought the bird down and held him out to Matthew.

'Tansy you *are* a bird person!' he said And Tansy had to agree.

EGMONT PRESS: ETHICAL PUBLISHING

Egmont Press is about turning writers into successful authors and children into passionate readers – producing books that enrich and entertain. As a responsible children's publisher, we go even further, considering the world in which our consumers are growing up.

Safety First
Naturally, all of our books meet legal safety requirements. But we go further than this; every book with play value is tested to the highest standards – if it fails, it's back to the drawing-board.

Made Fairly
We are working to ensure that the workers involved in our supply chain – the people that make our books – are treated with fairness and respect.

Responsible Forestry
We are committed to ensuring all our papers come from environmentally and socially responsible forest sources.

For more information, please visit our website at
www.egmont.co.uk/ethicalpublishing